I0450933

Miss Vee and Bee's Betrayal

Miss Vee Mysteries, Volume 3

Delilah Knight

Published by Corvid Moon Publishing, 2021.

MISS VEE AND BEE'S BETRAYAL

First edition. March 15, 2021.

Copyright © 2021 Delilah Knight.

ISBN: 978-1988688565

Written by Delilah Knight.

As always and with all my love, this book is dedicated to my mom and my husband. And to my real Miss Vee.

I would also like to acknowledge my editor, Cait Gordon, my cover designer, Nathan Fourchette, and my friends who believed in me.

Chapter One

We stood at the foot of an abandoned-looking grave. Aunt Bee had died only a couple of months ago, but her grave was already overgrown with weeds. The lack of a headstone didn't help. There was only a two-by-two-inch stick with a red flag and the code BL-N2-104. Beatrice Lilley, North quadrant, Row 2, grave 104.

It was sad, made worse by the fact that she had been my favourite aunt. Plus, we now knew she'd been murdered. Why would anyone murder a ninety-four-year-old woman? If they wanted her dead, all they had to do was wait.

I leaned heavily on my walker; my hip burned in a line straight down my leg and wasn't planning on taking my weight until I rested it. I heard my mom clear her throat behind me. While we'd been getting along better in the last few weeks than we had in, well, ever, I didn't feel prepared for her to cry on me. Not when this was the first time she'd told me where Aunt Bee had been buried. She could cry over anything else, not this.

After I listened for muffled sobs and didn't hear any, I turned to check. She looked annoyed.

"Mom?"

She sighed deeply. "I don't know why you wanted to come out here. Honestly, Victoria, it's a mess and without a proper marker, it looks like she was a criminal who died in prison." She stepped away and looked up. "I think it's going to rain, which is just perfect."

I looked up at the fluffy white clouds and late summer sun. Why was I surprised that she was making the worst of things? Why had I wanted her to come with me?

"About the headstone—"

"Don't nag at me about it, Victoria. Her estate was supposed to pay for one, but it's still tied up in that unending murder trial. You know I can't afford it on my pension. I don't know why they couldn't have let her be buried with dignity."

I closed my mouth. What to say first? That the trial of Bee's lawyer's killer was over, and the money was in the process of being released to my new estate lawyer? That I had the money that the killer hadn't managed to steal before being caught, so I *could* afford a stone?

"Ma, I—"

"Don't call me that. You sound like that family on the Sopranos."

I gritted my teeth and then breathed deeply, releasing the tension in my jaw. I'd faced down a killer; I could deal with my mother. "I have the money to buy a lovely headstone. In fact—"

"Then why don't you buy one and stop griping at me!" She turned and strode off through the graves, ignoring the paths, as they weren't a direct line out of the cemetery. She might be over eighty but acted younger than me. Her health was better, too.

I was willing to bet my favourite antique teacup that she'd drive off and leave me here.

It was a sucker bet. As I heard her car start up, I was glad I'd brought my cell. I'd need to call someone to get me home.

Victor leaned into my leg and whined, his least attractive habit. I looked down. He shivered in his baseball T-shirt; I should have brought him a sweater. The sun had moved behind a cloud, and my poor Chihuahua was still bald as my uncle Edgar. The vet said that his hair would grow back as his nerves settled, but I saw no sign of it.

"Guess you're right, we're stuck here."

I scooped him up to cuddle, and he licked the underside of my chin. I'd sort of stolen him from a killer who was mistreating him. Well, the police had thought he was mine at the time, so I didn't need to go into details with them, right?

A low rumble rose behind me, and I turned to see a large backhoe trundling toward me. At least Bee would have company soon.

MY NAME IS VICTORIA Lilley, and I'm a trans woman. There, I said it. I'm sixty years old, give or take, and I moved back to my hometown a couple of months ago when my aunt Beatrice left me her house and her money—ten million dollars! Currently, I had access to about a quarter of it, with most being tied up in locked deposits, trusts, and murder trials.

I sat on my rollator, holding Victor and watching the clouds scud across the sky. Maybe my mother had been right about the rain; they were moving fast.

Victor had settled down but still shivered every now and then. I would need to remember to keep a sweater for him in my oversized purse from now on. And a bottle of water to swallow my painkillers with. I had a prescription for extra-strong ones, but what use were they if I couldn't take them?

I was in serious need of one, too. I'd bruised the bone when I'd fallen onto a concrete floor, and my doctor had worried I'd damaged the fusion from when I was shot in that same hip. I just got out of the hospital day before yesterday from my *adventure* camping. Not that it had been advertised as such, but things had a tendency of happening around me.

How was I to know that there'd been bikers and criminals at the campground? And that Carl! Victor had growled at him from the moment we met. Maybe I should have listened to my dog. They say that they're great judges of character.

My stubbornness might also have had something to do with us getting caught up in everything. Not likely, but maybe.

I sighed. I could try being less stubborn and maybe listen to my friends more; Luci had wanted to leave the moment we'd arrived. She'd had a bad feeling from the start.

How long had I been waiting for Burt to show up? He'd seemed pleased I called him in my time of need, so why was he taking so long to get here?

I glanced at my watch. It had been less than twenty minutes. I shook my wrist and looked at it again, and it still lied to me. Did shaking work on digital watches? Would giving it a light smack work?

I sighed and glanced over to where the backhoe was digging, about twenty feet from me. They must dig even-numbered graves first, and then go back to do the odd-numbered ones. It seemed silly, but maybe the ground between the graves needed time to settle?

My watch now said twenty-two minutes. *Vanilla maple twist!* Time was moving so slow. At this rate, I'd still be here when the sun went nova.

IT SEEMED AS IF THINKING about him drew him out, as Burt materialized, turning the corner onto my path. Or Aunt Bee's path. He was still a ways away, but I felt better just seeing him.

He looked rather like a Santa's elf minus the tacky striped tights. Burt was short and round, already wrapped up in a bright-green puffy jacket. I could see a brownish scarf around his neck, which resolved into a black and red lumberjack plaid as he came closer.

"Hey, Vee! Hot enough for ya?" He laughed heartily at his own joke, which I didn't totally get. But he was cute for his age and was going out of his way to help, so I laughed too.

"Am I glad to see you! I'm about to get freezer burn out here." I stood up with a small jerk as my hip complained. Victor let out a muffled woof from my armpit.

Burt pulled a blanket out of a backpack I hadn't noticed and set it on my walker's seat for Victor. He was so thoughtful, if only he was twenty years younger. It was too bad that Aunt Bee had always rebuffed his courting, maybe he was open-minded.

Victor didn't want to leave my warm pit, but I insisted. I'd had enough cold wet nose for one morning.

Burt received a half-hearted lick in thanks for the blanket-from the dog, not me. *Heavens!*

Soon as he was wrapped up, Victor fell asleep. I guess all that shivering and whining wore him out. Burt helped guide my rollator to the gravel path. It wasn't ideal, but better than the grass had been, so I started moving slowly toward the cemetery entrance.

"So, what are you doing out here all alone, Vee? Contemplating your own mortality and the meaning of life?" He chuckled again.

"No, my mother brought me out to guilt me about Bee's lack of a headstone." I sighed. I wasn't being fair. "Now that the money from Bee's will is coming in, I can get her a really nice one. I'd hoped to discuss with mom over tea, but..."

"But Debs got huffy when you brought it up, right?" At my nod, he sighed. "Vee, girl, I spent a lot of time with Bee over the last few years. I heard all about her family, believe you me."

He paused to give my hip a few minutes rest and he pretended not to notice when I winced from moving my leg.

"Debs' problem is that she was the pretty one when they were young. Everybody thought she could do no wrong because she was such a delight to the eyes. By the time she grew up, that attitude had solidified into an expectation, so now she's terrified of being wrong."

I nodded. I'd never heard this part of Mom's history. We started walking without my really noticing; I hung on Burt's every word. I'd never imagined someone calling my mother Debs instead of Deborah. Whenever she said her name, you could hear the spelling, and she'd correct you if she heard Debra slip from your lips.

"She still tells people she's sixty," he added. "Can you believe that?"

I nodded; I'd heard her say that before. If I was her, I wouldn't claim a younger age, it emphasized how old you look. Me, I'm thinking of telling people I'm seventy-five. I look good for sixty, but I'd look fantastic for seventy-five. Plus, the added bonus of really annoying my mother.

I'd lost track of Burt's conversation, so I just nodded agreeably. Soon we were at the car.

I probably should have listened to Burt before being so agreeable. I wanted to go home and rest my leg but found myself parked in front of The Bun Journee instead. Well, I liked Ben a lot and his baking even more, so it wasn't a bad place to stop.

The Bun Journee is a small cafe belonging to my friend Benoit. *Bonne Journée* means "have a good day" in French, and is often said when leaving a conversation. I always loved a good food pun and had decided that this would be my favourite coffee shop the first time I saw it.

Plus, Benoit would be a sympathetic ear. He was no more impressed by my mother than Jaqi and Luci were.

That struck me as sad, all of a sudden. I needed a nice coffee to cheer me up. And maybe a maple-chocolate éclair. If Victor was right and being cold used calories, well, I had a few to spare.

Soon Ben had us all warm and cozy with cinnamon scented coffee, hot soup, and sweet cream pastries. I do love that man. If only I were thirty years younger, and he was he was into women.

And I wasn't that hard on the eyes: tall and lean, a swanky dresser if you loved the 1950s, and my hair in a cute pixie cut.

I breathed deeply and let my almost-sorta crush on Ben go. He was a happily married man, and I'd had it with romance.

Victor was the only male I'd let grace my bed again, even if he did fart in his sleep.

My phone rang, startling me out of my wandering thoughts. I glanced apologetically at Burt, but he was still consumed by his cream-filled éclair. He gestured at me to answer it, so I did.

"Hello?" It was Miko, Ben's husband. *Well, think of the devil and he will come.* Although Miko was no devil. Just the opposite, he was the only police officer in Smiths Falls that I respected. No, him and Constable Smith, whom I'd met once or twice. She seemed competent.

"Wait, what?" I pulled my attention back to the cell phone and Miko. "What was that about Aunt Bee?"

Miko sighed. "Vee, listen, this is important."

I nodded as if I expected him to see me. Didn't they have video phone calls now? We should do that in future. I realized there was silence on the line.

"Vee, when do you think I can come over?"

"For what?" I heard teeth grinding. *Butter ripple!* What was with my attention span today? "Miko? I'm in town just now. Why don't you drop over this afternoon before dinner?"

"Oh, you did hear me. Good. I'll be there about 4 p.m. if that's okay?"

I didn't hear him but agreed anyway. I didn't want to tell him I'd ignored him twice in one phone call. And how bad could it really be? Miko was a sweetie.

Chapter Two

The deck had been a relatively recent addition, built after Aunt Bee got too weak to walk to the park every day. She'd hired the boys upstreet to construct a large cedar deck with a porch swing, a table and chairs, a BBQ pit, and a small above-ground pool. The pool was just big enough to float on a lounger and sip wine. Or to do water aerobics, if you were so inclined.

I was not. Neither was she, and I smiled at the memory of the two of us floating side by side and nearly filling the pool.

It was a large deck, but there was still plenty of space left in the yard for grass and flower beds. Climbing roses grew along the edges of the white picket fence and, where the pagoda roof shaded the table, I'd planted grapevines.

It was late enough in the year that most of the flowers were gone, the tomatoes I had tucked in beside them were ripening, and the grapes were hanging down like a Renaissance painting.

I loved this deck. I placed my teacup and saucer on the glass-topped wicker plantstand along with a small plate of my favourite maple cookies. Victor immediately jumped up on the swing, and it started slowly moving back and forth.

Bee had built the porch swing herself, and it had sat under the lilacs for years. I remembered it from when I was still in high school. She'd used the frame from a swing set we'd all outgrown, and an old wicker love-seat with a broken leg. The loveseat hung by silver chains looped up and around the crossbeam of the swing set.

It creaked a little as I sat near my cookies and leaned back. I was tall enough to tuck one leg comfortably under me while the other touched the deck and kept the chair swinging lazily.

I'd always loved the aesthetics of a tall woman and was grateful for my height and strength. I loathed my thick wrists and ankles, though. I'd always wanted to be a delicate Fifties Girl like Mary Tyler Moore.

As I relaxed, I caught a whiff of lilacs and gardenia. The lilac trees shading the driveway hadn't bloomed since June, and gardenias weren't hardy this side of the U.S. border. It was Aunt Bee's perfume. I knew it was probably left on the cushions I'd sat on, but I took a sip of tea, closed my eyes and imagined that she'd come to visit.

I pictured her face, all crinkles from a lifetime of laughter. She'd have a coffee mug of tea; the china cups were too small for her. I smiled, I missed her so much.

A hand gently touched my arm, and I shrieked, tea flying everywhere. It was her ghost! I jumped up, spilling the last of my tea onto my white pants.

My eyes flew open to see Miko Shiomi standing in front of me, clutching his chest. It wasn't Bee. I felt oddly deflated despite being terrified a moment ago.

Miko had arrived a bit late. I'd left him a note to just come on through the house, but he'd walked around the house instead. That was why the sound of the door opening behind me hadn't given me warning that I wasn't alone anymore.

I patted my chest to still my thumping heart and smiled at Miko. We stared at each other until our breathing calmed, then he smiled crookedly at me.

"Feeling a little jumpy, Miss Vee?"

I sat and patted the seat next to me where Victor had already lapped up the spilt tea. Miko checked for wetness and sat down. His smile faded, his dark eyes turning somber.

"So, what can I do for you today? You need a date for the policeman's ball?" I grinned, knowing that there was no ball and, if there were, I would not be his date.

"We're excavating tomorrow, and I thought you might want to be there."

"Wait, what? Excavating what?"

He reached over to set his hand over mine. "The department has declared your Aunt Bee's death a homicide, Vee. There was no autopsy before because we thought it was natural causes. Now we have to exhume the body and perform one." He pulled a paper napkin from one of his many pockets and dabbed at the seat between us. "I thought you might want to be there, to make sure she's treated with dignity."

I nodded before even thinking about it. As he stood to go, handing me the napkin, I grabbed his hand.

"Am I a suspect in this murder, too?"

He didn't answer; he just gazed around at the garden as if he'd never seen it before.

"Miko, what's going on?"

He turned his head back toward me but not quite far enough to see me. Unless he had superhero peripheral vision, he just wanted to give the impression he was looking at me.

"You were her major heir, Vee. You inherited millions. Some people think that's suspicious." His hands raked through his hair, making it stand on end like a cartoon.

"You don't—" I cleared my throat to get rid of the slight quaver I heard in my voice. "You don't think I killed her, do you?"

He shook his head. "Doesn't matter, I'm not in charge of the investigation. MacGuinty is, and you know him."

Yeah, I knew him—loud, phobic, lazy... a worse cop I'd never met. He'd been positively eager to arrest me for the last murder.

"How did she die? I thought she fell down the stairs." I turned my head as he turned to face me.

"Sleeping pills. She'd overdosed on sleeping pills. That's why she fell."

I spun to face him. "Bee never took those. She slept like a baby." But a sinking feeling told me there was no way to prove that.

Miko shook his head, "I know. We already checked with her doctor and all three pharmacies in town. They weren't her pills."

I thought about it. I'd had a prescription for sleeping pills right after I started hormone therapy. I'd needed them for a couple of months until everything settled down. Taking those hormones had put me into instant menopause. Hot flashes, sleepless nights and everything.

But should I tell Miko about those pills? The prescription was over five years old, and I think I threw them away ages ago.

In the end, I kept silent.

THAT NIGHT WAS SUPPOSED to be a quiet one. I threw a store-bought frozen lasagna into the oven and opened a bottle of wine. I didn't even set the table; I was in the mood to eat in front of the TV, which is rare for me.

So, of course, the doorbell rang repeatedly. People had seen the cop car outside my house for over half an hour and wanted to know what was going on. After a while, when it seemed that pretty much everyone I'd ever met had arrived, I heard the oven timer ping.

One little lasagna would not feed this crowd, and no-one had brought anything. *Pot-stickers in gravy! Hm, Chinese food works better than ice cream flavors as a curse alternative.* That had really felt quite satisfying.

I debated sitting down and eating despite these unexpected guests, but my mother didn't raise me that way, so I left it in the now turned-off oven. Thank heavens for oven timers that worked.

By the time I returned to the parlor, Greta had organized the group, and they were all seated. They were also staring at me, dressed in my tea-stained linen. *Well, turnip cakes!* I'd never thought to put my slacks in cold water. Now that stain would set for sure.

By the time I got back from setting them to soak, Helen and Greta had made an open place for me on the long sofa. Right between Greta and Burt. One was cold and proper, the other too friendly. *Lovely.*

So, I explained what Miko wanted while my dinner cooled in the kitchen. I felt defeated, so tired of today. I wondered if I could get a do-over. Maybe, if everyone went home, so I could eat and go to bed.

Fortunately, I didn't say that out loud. They meant well, and it meant the world to me that they'd stepped up and welcomed me after Aunt Bee's death.

Which brought me out of my thoughts and back to the furious whispering.

Helen shook her head sadly, "I just can't believe it. An overdose. Do you think she…" She shook her head again, unable to voice her worst fear.

"Killed herself?" Helen's sister Greta stated manner-of-factly. Greta was a big-boned woman, solid both in manner and build. I always thought of her as good pioneer stock, born two centuries too late. "No, Bee had too much sense for that. And she would have told us if something was wrong."

I nodded. Bee had been her usual, happy self the last time I'd seen her.

"But, Greta, the only other possibility is that someone killed her." Helen's voice was hushed, as if speaking the thought made it real.

I sighed again. I'd been circling this same drain since Miko had left. "Well, either way, we'll find out soon." I stood up. "Much as I hate to say it, my supper's getting cold, and I need to be up early tomorrow. The dis-internment is at six. I need to be there."

My voice cracked a little, and the group of friends all hurried to their feet, trying to hug me. I had a bit of a dry throat from the lack of tea in my hands, but if they wanted to think it was emotion, let them. Maybe they'd get out so I could have some wine.

Helen and Burt hugged me, Burt getting his hands lower than my waist again. I had to tell him I wasn't interested. I knew I wouldn't, though. I felt too sorry for him.

"Do ya need a bit of company tomorrow, girl? I'll be up at dawn anyways."

Plus, he did things like that.

Helen quickly offered to come too, and soon all of us had agreed to meet here at 5:15 a.m. and carpool.

At least I think we all agreed. I don't remember anyone asking my opinion. I smiled as I hustled them out the door. I was starving and desperate for a drink.

I'd need to be up by 4:30 a.m. Being this awesome took work. *Red dragon sushi rolls!* How do I get myself into things like this?

THE NEXT MORNING, I carried my coffee out onto the front porch. It was in my favourite travel mug, dark blue with cherry blossoms. I had thought it might cheer me up, but it didn't. I hadn't been able to eat a bite, so this coffee was all that kept me going.

The breeze carried a hint of Fall and roses. My antique Victoria rose bushes were still in bloom. A few pink blossoms peeked from between the large leaves. Aside from being named after me—at least Bee had always claimed they'd been—the flowers started off bright pink and faded to white over several weeks. So, the large bushes had many shades of pink and white at the same time. I loved them dearly.

The coffee was a special one I'd ordered online. It tasted of almonds and chocolate. No slight meant to Ben, but it was every bit as good as his coffee. Almost despite myself, my mood improved.

Victor looked adorable in his bright blue fisherman's sweater and yellow rain-boots. I had the matching yellow rain slicker in my bag.

My bag. What could I say? It was huge. It currently carried Victor's and my raincoats, my pills, a bottle of water, my wallet, a paperback romance, my phone, and a bunch of odds and ends from my purse.

I was glad that I'd bought it when I saw it on sale last week. All of this stuff would have been way too much for my normal, albeit over-sized, purse. This new one seemed to weigh as much as I did when I lifted it. I'd have to place it on my walker seat.

Then where would my cute little doggie sit? Those short legs of his didn't carry him far before wearing out. I couldn't carry him and push the rollator at the same time.

I was pulled out of my thoughts by a small blue car slowing down in front of the house. I didn't recognize it, not Burt's or the Bedriska sisters' vehicle. Burt had a great big truck that he needed a step-stool to get into. I smiled at the thought; he looked so funny trying to pull up the stool up behind him on a frayed rope so he could get out again where he got where he'd been headed.

Greta and Helen drove a big, white car. So, I could be forgiven for standing up to try to get a better view of the driver. After all, he was cruising slowly by my house. A lady must be careful these days.

My movement seemed to spook the driver, as they took off before I got a good look. Oh well, they were probably looking at house numbers. I put them out of my mind as Burt strolled over, dressed once more in his poofy coat.

Chapter Three

We stood by the grave, a silent and somber group. Helen and Burt had both packed coffee thermoses, so we kept warm despite the wind and slight drizzle.

I could smell wet dog and wet wool. Not a great combination, but Victor had danced sideways when I tried to put his rain slicker on him. I suppose it could get hot in there with the sweater, but now both pooch and garment were wet. I, of course, had put on my pale aqua raincoat with no fussing whatsoever. Victor had remained unimpressed and refused to follow suit.

Everyone had brought umbrellas and I imagined that we looked like a Roman legion doing that shield-wall thing. Only prettier.

As the big digger-truck (I really must remember what they're called) rolled up, a lanky figure in a black frock coat hopped off of its fender by the driver. It had to be Father Murdock, the priest at Greta's church.

He wiped his damp hair off of his high forehead and walked quickly toward us. The woman from the other side of Burt's, whose name I never heard, greeted him cheerfully.

Who was she and why was she here? She didn't ride in with us; I would have noticed another body crammed into Helen's backseat.

She introduced him around, and he held my hand a bit too long. I put it down to sympathy, but something set my hackles up. Bee hadn't attended church at all the last few years. The last time was at the Baptist church on the edge of town. Why was he here?

"It's a bad business, Miss Lilley, very bad." He nodded as he said this as if emphasizing what his monotonous voice couldn't. "I'm Father Murdock, like the detective except I help solve the holy mysteries." He chuckled. I didn't join in. After a moment, his smile disappeared, and he continued talking. "I'm happy to assist you in this personal crisis, should you need someone to talk with."

How presumptuous. I'd never set foot in his church, wasn't Catholic, and had friends of my own. Why, there were half a dozen of them here right now.

I was saved from finding something to say to him by Ben's arrival, in company with Miko, and immediately following them came Lieutenant MacGuinty and a constable in a damp uniform. Miko simply nodded at Ben and headed for the grave. The big men stood there, smoking. MacGuinty made an "I'm watching you" gesture and stomped off to stand beside Miko.

A heavenly scent of vanilla, cinnamon and ginger distracted me from protesting about MacGuinty. Ben had brought food.

I SAT ON MY WALKER seat with Victor on a towel by my feet. The cold and damp had quickly settled into my right hip, starting up a slow throb.

Ben refilled my coffee with a flourish and handed me an almond croissant. Victor whined, but half-heartedly. He knew he didn't get people-food, no matter how good it smelled.

After what seemed a long time, the big man pushed himself up into the machine's cab and started the motor. Miko and the Lieutenant stepped away from the grave.

The machine backed up and aligned itself with where the casket must be. I was glad the headstone hadn't been placed yet; this was hard enough to watch without worrying if they would damage the stone.

The bucket was lowered slowly to one end of the plot as it was pulled forward; the teeth skidded across the grass for a moment, then dug in.

My heart pounded. I knew that this was necessary, but every fiber of my being protested disturbing Aunt Bee's rest. Father Murdock laid his hand on my shoulder; it felt oddly hot and uncomfortable. I knew he meant it as a kindness, but it wasn't. I felt a chasm open between us.

Ben eased closer, moving the priest away from my side. He held up the thermos he'd brought, but I'd had enough coffee. I felt jittery. He crouched beside me, careful to keep his knees out of the wet grass.

"How are you holding up, Vee?" His voice was soft, you could hear his sincerity. I nodded. I was okay, not great, but okay.

I couldn't look away as the bucket scraped noisily across something in the grave. It seemed too soon, how deep did they dig?

Miko waved at the driver and the engine cut out. The silence was heavy. Suddenly the clouds ripped open and rain fell like a solid curtain. In seconds, Victor's towel was soaked. He whined, and I put him on my lap, making sure that his paws were on the raincoat, not my slacks. I felt a headache start behind my eyes and my hip picked up the pace on its throbbing.

I watched in combined grief and fascination as they jumped into the pit and wrestled large straps around its contents. Miko was gesturing and from the look on his face, he wasn't happy. A roll of thunder drowned out his voice as shouted something to the men in the pit.

My friends crowded closer, drawn together by shared umbrellas and morbid curiosity. Suddenly, I wanted to get away, far away. My breath hitched and I felt... desperate? Afraid?

I turned to say something to Ben but was interrupted by the creaking of the straps, heard over the rain.

I glanced back toward Miko in time to see the first bit of Bee's coffin rise out of the dirt. The pouring rain and grumbling thunder made it a scene from a horror movie. All we needed was Prince Edward Island's red clay to finish it. It would look like that gothic movie about the red clay under a house...

My thoughts slowed, everything slowed.

I heard Miko shouting at someone to be careful. The straps creaked louder, and then one snapped with a sound like a gunshot.

The casket swung wildly, people near it running out of its way. It hit the ground on one corner and paused. Even the thunder held its breath.

Then it shattered.

Wood seemed to explode as the straps flew up and hit the machine's roof. I heard a man yell as he fell into the hole. Burt swore a blue streak, and Father Murdock even yelled, "Mother of God!" It might have been a prayer, but it struck me as a curse.

As Aunt Bee spilt out onto the grass and slowly slid into the hole with the constable, it struck me that this whole idea was cursed.

We should have let her rest.

Darkness closed in, and I heard Victor whine.

Chapter Four

I woke up to Victor licking my face. I hoped it was Victor because the breath that went with the rough tongue could peel the paint of a car.

Scratch that, I just hoped it was Victor—because licking.

I opened my eyes and realized I lay on the ground. Wet ground. In a graveyard.

That was it; I reached out a hand to the crowd circled above me and muttered, "Give me a hand."

No one did.

I tried to sit up, but Miko pushed me back down, a frown marring his pretty features.

"Don't move, Vee. You fainted." I saw a few heads nod.

"Ridiculous. I never faint. Help me up, I'm getting soaked." I pushed at a silvery blanket that had appeared, covering my legs, but it was too short for the rest of me.

After flopping like a fish for a few moments, Ben and Miko took my hands and pulled me to my feet. My hip spasmed, and I nearly fell again with only the force of my refusal keeping me up.

That and Ben's arm around my waist.

They moved me to sit on my walker again, and Victor danced around my feet before settling down on the silver blanket. I vaguely recognized it as one of those emergency blankets from the hardware store. I missed the days that emergency responders brought blankets that were real wool. That piece of tin foil just wasn't the same.

Burt's voice penetrated my tumbling thoughts.

"Should we call an ambulance?" He waved his hand in my face. "She must've hit her head. Is she bleeding?"

Hands probed my scalp, and I pushed them away.

"I'm perfectly fine, I was just a touch shocked by Aunt Bee..." The exploding casket and Bee's graceless tumble back into her grave came back to me. I must have paled because Miko shoved my head down toward my knees.

I slapped his hands away. Glaring at him, I pulled my dignity around me like a cloak. "I said I'm perfectly fine. What happened to Aunt Bee?"

Miko's face fell with both embarrassment and shame. Ben pressed a cup of coffee into my hands, and I had to admit the heat was comforting.

"We'll get it... the bucket damaged the top of... don't you worry about it. I'll make everything right, Vee."

I wondered how. But I'll admit, I was glad of him taking charge, there was no way I wanted to go look at the mess this dis-internment had become. Handled with dignity, my skinny white butt.

Miko's face pinked, and I realized I'd said at least the last part out loud. I shook my head and reached over to pat his arm.

"It's okay, sort of. But I can't watch anymore. I want to go." The last came out almost in tears. Okay, so maybe I was more upset than I thought.

Just thank the Lord my mother hadn't been here.

Crap. I'd forgotten to call her. She needed to know. At least the bare details.

I could leave all the drama out of it.

Hah! Leave out the drama. With my mother.

At least that thought made me smile.

I NOTICED MACGUINTY laughing at the poor constable stuck down the hole. How rude. And how callous. He knew that was my aunt and that I was sitting right here. If I could've disliked him more, I would. All I could do is turn my back on him and try to pretend he wasn't there.

The group said they were going to take me back to the Bun Journee, but I was so coffeed out, I just wanted to go home. Neither Burt nor Helen would hear of it, though. They acted like dropping me off at my lovely little bungalow was the same as dropping me into the pit of despair.

I might have whined a little, or it might have been Victor. Somehow we ended up at the Viking Hoard, a bar-restaurant that specialized in, well, Vikings. Scandinavian food, drink and decorations, it reminded me of that TV show.

What was it with all of the themed restaurants and cafes in this town? When I was growing up, the only place with a theme was a strip club outside of town: Girls, Girls, Girls. And it wasn't so much a theme as a description.

Since I wouldn't leave Victor in the car (and really, who does that?), we ended up seated on the patio, under a huge blood-red umbrella. The rain had tapered off to a mild drizzle, though it was still damp. Victor huddled under my chair, shooting pathetic glances at Burt until he caved and moved him to an empty chair.

A cute blond man with a medievalist tunic brought us ice water and menus. I grabbed my painkillers from my purse to take one. To be honest, I dug around, cursing under my breath until I found them, then I took one.

I didn't listen as he reeled off the specials and ordered a gin martini with a curl of lime. Unless it was the fancy gin in the blue bottle, that brand tasted better with cucumber. Burt ordered a local beer and the sisters asked for tea.

They missed the point of taking me to a bar, bless their hearts, but whether it was 5:00 p.m. or not, I needed a drink.

It turned out that Viking Hoard had a very similar menu to the Swedish Store in Ottawa, but with a few additions.

I couldn't imagine eating a savory and spiced porridge, although the lamb stew with barley dumplings and cream gravy sounded interesting. So did the pork stew with potatoes and cabbage, but I decided to avoid cabbage for the sake of the other people in the car.

The sisters played it safe with poached salmon and mashed potatoes, Burt opted for the sausage and cheese plate with crusty bread. I decided on the stew. And another drink.

My hands were a little chilly and everything cooled far too fast, but the food was really good. The lamb was garlicky and well balanced by the herbed gravy. The dumplings were a bit chewy and seemed to have seeds or something in them. Odd but delicious.

So, I was feeling quite a bit better by the time I decided that I couldn't put off talking to my mother any longer.

They dropped me off at home, the cowards. Even Burt said he was not facing my mother with this news. So much for being able to handle *Debs*.

Between the prescription pain pills and the gin, I was pretty confident I could handle her. Nothing that happened had been my fault, not the autopsy, not the unburial, and certainly not Bee's swan dive into the hereafter.

Maybe I should sober up before I call? No, I'll take the liquid courage.

She didn't answer her phone. Figures.

I WAS DOZING IN MY lounger when my cell phone rang, nearly sending me through the roof. It flew out of my hands and disappeared among the couch cushions.

It continued to ring as I hobbled over and searched the blanket and pillows, stopping just as I found it. *Fudge crackle!*

I poked at buttons until I found the one that gave me my call history. It was my mother. Call her right back or wait a bit and pretend I'd been in the bathroom? It meant a lecture either way, so I went to put the kettle on. I needed a nice Darjeeling to fortify me.

The tea was insufficient, so I called Luci first. She's half of the happy couple who are my besties. They live about an hour away, in Ottawa. I used to rent their spare room but moved here after inheriting the house.

Luci always spoke from her heart; she'd have good advice on dealing with this situation. Maybe she'd drive down to back me up.

As she puts it, she'd *have my twelve*. That should have been *have my six*, but Luci had pointed out that there are two of us, and if we have each other's six, that makes twelve.

I was stalling again, so I just poked her photo in my contact list, and the call started ringing on her end.

"Hello, my Vee, how are you doing?" Her voice was warm and happy, and I relaxed instantly. Her soft Spanish lilt had that effect on people.

"Sweetie, it has been a day, let me tell you." So, I did. She responded with all the right noises and murmured sympathy until I got it all out.

"Do you want me there?"

I shook my head, "No, you don't have to. It's a long drive." I did want her here, but I wasn't feeling right about bothering her all of a sudden. This was my problem, not hers.

"I did not say do you need me to fix it for you. I asked if you wanted me." Lucia's voice was mildly chiding, and I knew I'd been thinking out loud again.

"I know, sweetie. But I just don't want to bother you."

She laughed, "Your mother will be no bother. She likes me." Her voice muffled, and I heard voices on the other end. I knew she had put her hand over the phone and was talking to her partner, Jaqi.

I waited for her attention to return to me so I could tell her to forget it. Instead, Jaqi came on the line.

"Hey, Vee. This isn't dangerous is it? I mean, they're just investigating to see if Aunt Bee died of natural causes, right?"

I love Jaqi like a sister. A sister I couldn't lie to. Not that I lied to my sister Karey on a regular basis, it was just that if I said it was safe and it wasn't, Jaqi might never forgive me.

"They already know she was murdered, well, they strongly suspect it. But it's not involving me, not really. Not the investigation, I'm just feeling so adrift. Like everything is wrong, you know?"

"Yeah, I do." There was a bit more muffled muttering. "Okay, we can come down for a few days. Long enough to help you get Aunt Bee settled again. When do you want us?"

"Now?" I heard a quaver in my voice and blinked rapidly to avoid tearing up.

So, they agreed to be here in a couple hours and told me to do nothing until they arrived. Easier said than done.

About a half-hour later, my phone rang again. I assumed it was Jaqi, so I answered right away. It was not Jaqi.

"Victoria, why do I always have to hear these things from other people? Your fingers aren't broken, you could call."

"Hello, mother." So much for waiting for Lucia to act as a buffer. "How are you today?"

"How am I? How do you think I am when I have to hear on the gossip news line that Bee's been dug up?" Her voice rose in tone and volume the more she spoke. Soon only Victor would be able to hear her.

"Mom, calm down, it wasn't that bad." I crossed my fingers.

"And were you there? Did you really tell them to dig her up?" Her voice was almost shrill enough to cut glass. So, I put a hand over my glasses to protect them, and maybe prevent a migraine from forming, and strove to remain calm.

"Mom. Let me explain." I could hear her breathing, but she wasn't talking, so I grabbed a deep breath and told her about the lab results and the need to perform an autopsy. She was still silent, so I gave a much-edited version of the events at the gravesite this morning.

Lord in heaven, had it only been this morning?

Silence fell heavy on the line. I decided to outwait her. There we were, each waiting for the other to say something. We would have remained like that forever if there hadn't been a knock on my door.

"Someone's at the door, Mom. I have to go."

"Don't you dare drop this on me and hang up. Tell them to come back later."

I peered through the curtains to see the sisters Bedriska standing on the porch. Unfortunately, Greta spotted me, so I couldn't pretend I wasn't home.

I opened the door, waving the phone at them so they could hear my mother's tinny voice.

"Mom, I have to go, the ladies from upstreet are here."

"I told you-never mind, I'll be there in a few minutes." The call ended with a beep.

Well, spiced vanilla fudge crackle with lemon drops!

I tried to smile at Greta, but she just scowled back. Helen elbowed her in the waist, about as high as she could reach.

"May we come in, dear?" Helen was such a contrast to her big, and bigger, sister. I hate to say it, but she reminded me a bit of a chicken. Her eyes were small and dark, her neck had a wattle, and her movements were quick and nervous. Greta was about a foot taller, blue-eyed and raw-boned. I didn't have the nerve to ask if they were really sisters, and it was none of my business really.

Which just made me burn to ask, of course.

The awkward silence reminded me that I hadn't answered, and I hurried to assure them that they were welcome to come in. I headed to the kitchen to put the kettle on again while they settled themselves in the parlor.

I was curious about why they had come but more worried about mom's arrival than about the ladies on my sofa. What would I say to her? What if the sisters were still here, what would Greta say?

The very thought made me rush the tea a little, and hurry back to them.

They just quietly waited, like the crows in the Alfred Hitchcock movie. I forced a smile.

"Who would like some tea?"

After fussing with the cups and handing out my maple cream cookies, we stared at each other. After a short but uncomfortable silence, Greta took charge.

"We all saw what happened to dear Beatrice this morning."

I nodded. Had she missed me fainting and Ben screaming?

"I believe that she needs a proper re-internment to help her rest after that disgrace," Greta added.

Helen nodded. I blinked. I wasn't aware of her being the restless dead. Or even the unhappy dead.

But Greta nodded firmly. "There must be a mass said over her grave. I have already spoken with Father Murdock."

"Well, that was pretty bold of you." I was unreasonably upset by her actions, I knew that. But I'm not Catholic and neither was Aunt Bee, she only paid lip service to church matters. And she was *my* aunt, not Greta's. She had no right.

Before I could say something unfortunate, the doorbell rang and in walked my mother.

Peppermint-crackling fabulous.

MY MOTHER. EIGHTY-FIVE years old, straight-backed as a drill sergeant, dainty as bird, terrifying.

She opened the door and strode in like she owned the place. Not a white hair was out of place in her sweeping updo; her makeup was flawless in shades of pink and tea rose. How did she do that?

I rose and hurried over to her, and she met me with a judgy look and air kisses. It was one of those days. I reminded myself that Beatrice had been her sister-in-law, and she had a right to be upset.

More of a right than Greta, now that I thought about it.

I led Mom to the wing-back chair opposite mine. Its strange pastel teal colour flattered her while making me look yellow. She came to a full stop before sitting down, staring at Greta and Helen.

"Mom, these are the Bedriska sisters from upstreet. They would like to plan something for Bee's re-internment." I smiled hopefully.

Mom sniffed as she regarded Greta, unapproving of her poor decision to grow large and strong. I could see Greta's hackles rise.

"Ladies," I interjected before my mom said anything cutting, "I'd like you to meet my mother, Deborah Lilley. Mom, can I get you anything? Tea, coffee, a baseball bat?"

She shifted her disapproving stare to me. "Why would I want a baseball bat?"

I had no answer, it had just slipped out.

Fortunately, she was distracted by Greta, who, having no sense of danger or self-preservation, asked my mother's opinion on having a mass read at Bee's graveside.

"A mass? You mean Catholic?" Mom turned to stare at me incredulously. "Was this your poor idea, Victoria? There is nothing I think less appropriate."

I shook my head. "I don't think the priest would like it either."

"And why not? He was there to see the shambles that was made of her unburial." Greta's face pinked a bit.

"That's not a word," My mother and Helen said in unison. This earned Helen a nod of approval.

That reminded me. "Why was the priest even there?" I asked.

"I invited him," Greta said loudly. "I felt that something so distasteful as digging up a grave should be blessed by the church."

She held her head up, a challenge in her eyes. One that my mother was only too happy to meet.

Before I could say anything to head off the oncoming catfight, Helen leaned over and placed a hand on my mother's clenched fist.

"We didn't mean to overstep, Mrs. Lilley, and I apologize. It's just that Bee was such a dear friend and her loss so difficult for us. Then this unpleasant business..." Tears filled her eyes and melted my mother's anger away.

Mom patted Helen's hand and smiled softly. "She was a wonderful woman. But we are Baptist, and Bee had a lovely service at the funeral."

Greta opened her mouth, but the doorbell rang before she could get a word out.

I hurried to open the door, thanking whatever god was up there for the interruption. I didn't even care who it was.

It was Burt.

"Burt! What are you doing here? Is something wrong?"

He smiled, his eyes crinkling with mischief. "I saw the sisters arrive and figured you'd need saving about now."

He pulled off his navy toque and scarf and tossed them onto the bench I kept by the door. Technically, the bench was for sitting on while you removed your boots, but it was piled with hats, gloves, Victor's sweaters, and such.

Burt headed into the parlor like he lived here. I wasn't sure if I was glad to see him or not.

I heard him greet everyone as I stood there with the door open. I didn't want to go back in. I didn't want to think about Bee's graceless descent from her casket, or hear people argue over who missed her the most. And I certainly didn't want to pretend to be happy to see everyone when all I wanted to do was curl up and mourn my aunt.

Tea. I could buy a few minutes by making more tea. I knew it wouldn't win me more than that, I was expected to play hostess and whatnot. Some days I wished I wasn't such a lady and could just toss everyone out on their ears.

While waiting for the water to boil, I heard the doorbell ring and the door open. *Jumping Jehoshaphat!* Was the whole neighborhood meeting here?

I peered around the corner, searching for the courage to ask everyone to leave. It was Jaqi and Lucia.

I nearly cried; I was so glad to see them. Jaqi could handle the sisters, and Luci could melt the coldest heart, meaning, my mother.

Coward that I am, I shouted hello and went back to the kitchen. Well, the water was nearly boiling, so I had to make tea. Right?

I fiddled with a bag of cookies, trying to decide if I wanted to lose the entire bag to the crowd in the parlor. Oh, I knew I could always buy more, but shopping was no longer the joy it had been before busting up my hip.

In the end, conditioning won out over greed, and I plated the cookies up and brought them out with the tea. The cream and sugar were still on the coffee table from the last pot, so I just had to bring out extra cups. I was grateful for Bee's collection of tea trays.

The parlor was eerily quiet. I could feel the hairs on my neck stand up. What had I missed? What sight would greet me in there—dead bodies? Had they all killed each other?

I was equal parts relieved and disappointed to see everyone sitting and listening to Burt talk about a trip he'd taken with Bee a few years ago.

His soft voice rose and fell as he described the autumn leaves and his hopes for a romantic getaway being dashed as Bee booked separate rooms. My mom smiled.

Only half of the people here knew my aunt had been trans, like me. And that half didn't include Burt or the sisters. We really didn't need that conversation right now. Or ever, as far as I was concerned.

I cleared my throat to stop anyone from explaining it and started to walk to the coffee table. Burt leaped up mid-sentence to take the tray from me. Now if only there was an empty chair to sit on.

Burt offered me his, but I was reluctant to take it. So, Luci moved to the arm of my chair and gestured for me to sit. I ignored my mother's disapproving look and just gestured for people to help themselves. Tea was not the hill I was willing to die on.

SOON, PEOPLE'S MOUTHS were too full of my favourite cookies to talk crap or argue, so the mood mellowed. Tea does that.

Luci wiped a few crumbs from her shirt and smiled at my mom.

"Mrs. Lilley, what would you think of a nice memorial when Aunt Bee is re-interred? We could bring her favourite things and talk about our favourite memories of her. Then maybe have a picnic at the park next door."

Burt and Helen perked up. So, did I. It was a lovely thought and didn't involve religion.

Mom made a show of thinking about it, but I could tell she liked the idea. Finally, she nodded.

"As long as you don't try to turn it into another funeral or a Catholic mass." She shuddered on the last word, and I hurried to say something before Greta could reply.

"I have a lot of Bee's favourite tea here. And Ben could make her almond croissants for the picnic. We should invite him. He misses her, too."

Jaqi pulled out paper and a pen. "Who should we invite? And when is the re-internment? Have you heard from the police yet?"

Greta had looked like she was about to speak, but the last line deflated her. It reminded us that Bee had been murdered. Mom put her teacup back on the table beside her.

Jaqi was scribbling on her pad as if she hadn't even noticed the sudden chill. Maybe she hadn't. She did tend to become totally involved in what she was doing. A list isn't really writing, but there were a lot of things to write down.

I peered over her shoulder where she sat at my feet. She had pretty much everyone I could think of listed, I just asked her to add my sister, Karey.

Then I had a thought. The weekly neighborhood potluck would be a good time to plan things. Like who brought what for the picnic. I know it's not really a potluck if you plan it, but who wanted five bowls of salad?

Burt offered to bring beer for everyone, but mom put the kibosh on that. So Jaqi offered wine, which suited my mother's delicate sensibilities much better. Burt shrugged, and I knew he'd bring beer for himself anyway.

Helen was making a list of neighbors she thought would want to be included, and Greta made sure Father Murdock was among them. Mother's lips pinched a bit, but she didn't say anything.

I just hoped that she wouldn't be too mean to him. In an odd way, this reminded me that Miko had said he'd been told Bee had a stalker.

It seemed as good a time as any; Mom was fairly relaxed and even Greta looked like she might not be horribly offended. So, I turned to Burt and asked.

"Burt, you said something to the police about Bee having a stalker when she died. What did you mean by that?"

Mom looked at me strangely as a flush crawled up Burt's neck.

"What a ridiculous notion. The woman was far too old for that nonsense," Greta said and huffed at Burt, and a stubborn look stole over his face.

"What makes you think there's an age limit on love?" Burt asked, shaking his head. "And I wasn't talking about me. There was someone else, made her nervous to get them letters."

"She couldn't have had two delusional old men sending her poetry. Face it; she wasn't that much of a catch," Greta said as she glanced at my mom and smiled thinly. "I mean, at her age. Men usually make fools of themselves over much younger women."

I agreed in principle, but Aunt Bee had been a special person, and I didn't like hearing it. Besides, Burt wouldn't have reported himself as a stalker. *Would he? No, he wouldn't.* His mind was clear enough to remember which notes he had written and could have recognized another's handwriting. *I hope.*

"What notes do you think were from someone else, Burt?" Helen's voice was soft, diffusing the anger hovering in the room.

Burt nodded, "There was one I remember. She hurried over to show it to me soon as the mail arrived." He took a breath and squinted, as if reading from a letter in his mind. "You can't have what's mine. Do you think I wouldn't notice you stealing everything from me? Give it up before I take everything from you."

"That's no love poem." The words were out of my mouth before I even realized I was speaking. Burt nodded vigorously and Greta rolled her eyes.

"Of course, it is. You gave her your heart and she didn't love you. It's a threat from a bitter old man."

Chapter Five

The following day was bright and sunny without warming up. We'd decided—well, Greta had decided, and no one was able to change her mind—that the potluck was best held at the church.

My hip and Victor voted for indoors as opposed to sitting on the ground in someone's backyard, so it was settled.

I packed up my German potato salad with cheese and pickle bits in it and waited for Luci to arrive. Jaqi had bowed out on account of work, but I suspected she was saving her time off for the day of the reburial. Which would be Wednesday.

I'd finally gotten permission from the police. But since they'd been stingy with information and even Miko wasn't allowed to talk to me, I was in no rush to be nice to them. I politely told the coroner for the third time that Bee's re-internment was scheduled for Wednesday afternoon, and as I had no wish to store her in my fridge, I'd told the funeral home to pick her up Wednesday morning.

Now to wait for the test results.

A large part of me hoped the original test was wrong, and she had died of natural causes. But my head itched. I knew I was missing something.

It felt a little bit chilly as I sat on the porch, waiting for everyone to show. Soon it would truly be fall. Much as I loved the pumpkin spice everything and the cute sweaters and high boots, my hip didn't like being cold.

I wasn't too fond of it either. And Victor hated it. He had wiggled his way under my shawl, shivering despite the thick, dark green sweater he wore. And his little footsies were so cold.

I got up to go fetch him some warm slippers when a honk sounded at the edge of the street.

Seriously? A honk? *Who the raspberry ripple would dare honk at me?* I turned back and glared at the road. *I know, I know. Next I'll be yelling, "Get off my lawn!"*

But all I saw was the tail end of a blue car disappearing behind the hedge that separated my house from the next one. Must not have been honking at me after all.

Burt huffed his way across his lawn and my driveway, grinning when he saw me. He was sweet, but he'd had a crush on Bee, and ninety was just too old for me. However much he hinted at his youthful prowess. I wasn't her.

THE CHURCH HALL WASN'T as bad as I'd feared. A small crucifix hung on the wall opposite the door, the only thing to point out that this space usually had been a Sunday school.

It had a small kitchen with a six-burner stove, an all-fridge, and an upright freezer. I felt instantly consumed with envy. Never mind that I didn't cook much, this kitchen was amazing. It even had a lot of cupboards and counter space. If only it was bigger; there was barely room for three of us in prepping the food. I managed to fit three trays into the oven and set it to heat up. I couldn't guarantee an even heat, but they would all be ready at the same time.

Greta kept busy putting anything with eggs or milk into the fridge, and ice cream went into the beautiful freezer. I decided then and there that I would get a stand-up freezer, even if I had to put it on the deck.

Back in the main room, I could hear Burt organizing the chairs and greeting people. Luci leaned in the kitchen door and handed Helen another large cake. This one was covered in pink icing, so I couldn't really guess its flavor. I hated to even think it, but I hoped it wasn't another chocolate cake. We already had three.

This is why I like to plan potlucks.

I NIBBLED AT AN EXCEEDINGLY bland devilled egg and glanced around the room. I recognized only about half of the faces. From what I could overhear, most were talking about the weather or themselves. I wondered if they even knew Aunt Bee or had just come for the company and the food, which wasn't that great.

I put down the rest of the egg and looked for my sister, Karey. I spotted her over with mom and Luci, sitting by the dessert table. I made my way over, pausing to dump my leftovers in the garbage and set the plate in one of the buckets provided for that purpose. I felt sorry for whoever had to wash the dishes, but not sorry enough to volunteer. I'd already helped with preparing the food.

I pulled my walker up close to the little group and sat down. Luci immediately handed me a piece of chocolate cake on a napkin. I glanced at the table behind her to see five chocolate cakes, each missing a few slices. *I know chocolate was Aunt Bee's weakness, but seriously, folks.*

"This one is best." She grinned. "I made it."

I tentatively took a bite, but Luci was right, it was delicious. Moist, bright with cinnamon and orange, but still very chocolaty.

As I chewed happily, Aunt Kay arrived, carrying another cake. My mother rolled her eyes and got up to go meet her.

I took the opportunity to ask if either Luci or Karey knew when the conversation would move to Aunt Bee's memorial. Karey shook her head.

"I'm not sure it will unless we make an announcement. I don't think everybody understands that's why we're here."

Luci nodded and grinned impishly. "Ask your mother to lead the talk. She'll get it done so fast."

I laughed. Luci was right. And since Mom lived to be the center of attention, it wouldn't even occur to her that this was not her neighborhood. Karey and Luci high-fived as I turned to look for Mom and Kay.

They were in the kitchen. Perfect.

"You're Bee's sister," I said to Aunt Kay, "You should be the one leading the discussion. You know better than anyone what she would have wanted at her memorial."

Of course, my mother immediately responded. "Don't you think this situation is hard enough on her without putting her center stage for everyone to stare at?"

Kay nodded, and the bait was set. Mom was nosing around it, seeing if it was safe to take it.

"You are absolutely right, Mom. You should do it."

She peered at me to see if I was serious, and then demurred. She couldn't, there must be someone else more appropriate...

But both Kay and I knew Mom was dying to take over, so we told her what she needed to hear. After a few minutes of *convincing*, she happily took charge.

As I took Aunt Kay's German chocolate cake out to the table, I watched Mom walk straight to the head of the room, opposite the food tables and clap her hands to get everyone's attention.

As soon as she announced the theme of the discussion to follow the lunch, people began packing up and leaving. I knew that not everyone in the neighborhood was close to Bee, but really.

Within minutes, all of the dishes were either stacked to be washed or covered and taken home. The place emptied out faster than cathouse with a flea infestation.

Mom didn't seem to mind, though. She waved goodbye to a toddler tossed over Daddy's shoulder and headed back to us.

"There, now that the riff-raff is gone, we can get started." She glanced at the remaining desserts and shook her head. "Is anyone else expected?"

I glanced around. Father Murdock was helping himself to a few leftovers and chatting with Greta in the kitchen. Burt and Helen were tidying tables and clucking over the manners of people who just left their plates for others to deal with.

"Ben's not here yet," I said. He seemed to be the only one missing. "He said he'd show up after the lunch rush."

Mom looked at her watch. "It's after two, Victoria. How long do those people eat lunch?"

I gritted my teeth and smiled, that was a discussion for the ride home—not here. "Well, he owns the place. I imagine he's giving lunch breaks to the staff."

Mom sniffed but nodded. I'd count that as a win. Besides, I was pretty sure that her jab at Ben was habit, not actual distaste. Luci smilingly handed my mother a piece of her cake. She winked at me, and I knew that she was filling Mom's mouth so she couldn't talk.

There was a flurry of *Oh, I couldn't*, and *I'm watching my figure* before Mom settled down to eat it. Luci poured coffee for those who wanted it, and I decided to get started before my patience fled altogether from waiting. I hate waiting. And fiddle-fallying.

And I knew that the sooner we started, the sooner we'd finish. I hadn't been allowed to bring Victor because of Health Department rules and was concerned about the size of his bladder.

I needn't have worried; the discussion seemed to be helped by the addition of cake, not hindered. Ideas for Bee's ceremony flew fast and wild. I actually had to rein them in.

There was to be no horse-drawn carriage bringing her remains to the grave site. *We're not the Brontë sisters!*

But we all agreed that a potluck—an organized potluck—back at my place after the internment would be best. We could toast Bee with her favourite sweet sherry and share fond memories.

Father Murdock didn't say much, just agreed that everything was a grand idea, until we reached the question of a service. He and Greta were determined to have a mass said even though no one in the family wanted it. Trying to guilt-trip me was not a good choice.

"No disrespect intended, Father, but are you even listening? No. Mass. None." My mother waved her hand at me to shush me, more because I was being rude than anything else. "Aunt Bee wasn't Catholic, I'm not Catholic, her sister isn't Catholic, no one in the family is Catholic. You're pretty much it. So, no mass."

He gritted his teeth and glared at Greta. It occurred to me that she may have gotten the church hall today by promising a mass. *Oops.*

Luci waved her fingers at me. She was Catholic, too. *Double oops.*

I tried to be a bit conciliatory, but I wasn't sure he appreciated the effort. "Father Murdock, Aunt Bee already had a church funeral, and I'm sure her soul is well situated. This is more of a memorial for those of us who didn't make it to the funeral. Maybe just say a few nice words?"

In the end he sorta tossed us out, pointing to the dirty dishes and mentioning there was another event that day. I was sure I'd hear about that later.

Just as the last of us closed the Hall door, Ben's pink catering van pulled up. Crap, I'd forgotten all about him.

"Oh, sweetie, am I too late? I brought chocolate cake."

"Mom, you remember Ben. He owns the Bun Journee down by city hall." Mom shook his hand and nodded. I could tell by the look on her face that she had didn't connect him to *"gay Ben"* we'd talked about earlier. *That's okay, I'm not twelve. My mother doesn't have to approve my friends.*

Yet, by the time everyone made it to their cars; Mom acted like he was her best friend. Ben had that effect on people.

MIKO HAD PLANNED TO meet us at my place by supper, so I hustled everyone home. My home, not theirs. Greta had left in a huff when Father Murdock rushed us out, but Helen cadged a lift from Luci, and we all made it back before Victor's bladder burst.

Though I'd guess it was a near thing based on how fast his little legs ran out the door and onto the lawn. He didn't even pause to bark at anyone.

Burt offered to stay with him so I could put the kettle on. He looked like he was chewing over something sour, so I let him. Normally, I would have just called Victor back into the house, but if Burt needed to stew, I'd let him stew. I'd know what it was about soon enough.

When Burt came back in, he had Greta with him. Her snit seemed to have worn off.

My parlor resembled a mall on Christmas Eve—no room to move, and God help you if you need to get to the washroom. We'd even dragged in the dining room chairs to make seats for everyone. Of course, this took up all my floor space and nobody could get up out of their seat for fear of falling into someone else's lap. I hoped everyone had bigger bladders than my poor dog.

I toyed with my teacup, I'd put out the good china because Mom was here, but she didn't seem to notice. She and Kay had withdrawn into the corner loveseat and murmured to each other.

I could hear Ben in the kitchen, busting a gut laughing at the remains of five different chocolate cakes, six counting his.

We hardly had to wait at all for Miko to show up. And from the look on his face, he had news. Good thing he liked to stand up when he talked, there wasn't a chair in the house for him to sit on.

Miko stood in the parlor doorway and looked over the crowd with eyebrows raised. A good hostess would have gotten up to give him her seat. I was not a good hostess.

I was somewhat hemmed in by Luci sitting on the floor by the coffee table, though she would have moved out of the way, I'm sure. But I'd had a long few days, and I was bone-deep tired. I'd talked to so many people, I was talked out, and that never happens.

Not that I wanted to be rude, either. So, I wiggled my butt to the edge of the chair and started to stand. My hip flared like a supernova of pain, and I gasped. Miko immediately waved at me to stay seated.

Luci gave me a scolding glance, and even Victor cocked his head to stare at me, so I slid back.

Miko cleared his throat and crossed, then uncrossed his arms.

"I assume everyone here knew Beatrice Lilley." There were nods around the room. Miko drew a deep breath as my mother caught and held his gaze. He nodded slightly to her, and she looked away. I wondered what that was about.

"The police have determined that Miss Lilley's death was not an accident." He raised his voice over the mutters of fake surprise. "Does anyone have any information that might help us with a suspect list? Did anyone see or hear anything unusual?"

The mutters grew louder, and I caught a snatch of Burt cussing. So did Miko, as he pointed at Burt and asked his name.

Which he didn't exactly give.

"I live on the other side of the driveway. And Bee's death had to be an accident. She was a lovely woman; no one could have hurt her." His eyes shone, with tears or passion, I wasn't sure.

But Miko shook his head. "I understand how you feel, mister-" Burt just crossed his arms and glared. Miko shrugged. "Our tests were conclusive; this was a homicide. What I need is anyone who knows or saw anything that could help us to come forward. Privately, not here."

He jerked his chin toward the kitchen, and I leaned forward to put Victor on the floor so I could follow him. In front of me, my mother rose gracefully from the dining room chair she'd been sitting on and followed him out.

What could my mother know? I itched to follow them both but was still hemmed in. Plus, my hip still hurt. I'd overdone it at the church hall.

As soon as my mom's trim backside was out the door, the noise level rose precipitously. A fancy way of saying, "Holy spumoni, can these people talk loudly!"

I overheard Helen chastising Burt for something, likely for not mentioning the threatening note. Greta's voice rode roughshod over all the others as she ordered us, *ordered us*, not to discuss what we knew until after talking with the police. Well, that did not help. Everyone just got louder.

I felt a spike of pain behind one eye from the noise, the lack of air from so many people in such a small room, and my renewed sorrow brought up by the memorial talks and Miko.

I just wanted to be alone to lie down. Instead, I hugged Victor and breathed in his doggy smell. After a moment, I leaned back in my chair and laid my head back, closing my eyes. *Go away,* I thought to myself. Of course, no one did.

And nobody solved anything either. Just the same talking points... lovely woman... can't believe this... miss her... stalker... soon my thoughts started to buzz softly despite the racket.

Victor startled me back from the edge of sleep by barking and trying to climb over me to get to the window. In that short period of relaxation my hip had stiffened up, and I winced as I turned to see what Victor was after.

I saw nothing. No squirrels, no people, not even a car going past. That reminded me of the car this morning, and I turned back to the room.

"Who owns the Wedgwood-blue sedan?" The volume dipped as those who could hear me turned toward me. I dropped Victor onto the floor again, and he practically dove under the curtain to look outside.

Helen shrugged and looked at Greta. She also shrugged. Burt offered that he'd seen one the other day but had no idea whose it was. "Probably someone from way upstreet."

I didn't think so. In fact, the more I thought about it, the more convinced I was that the car had slowed down to honk at me.

Oh, my shoes and stockings! Could it be Bee's stalker? Then one voice rang clear over the crowd. My Aunt Kay.

"I wonder if this has to do more with Brian than Beatrice. He did abandon..." She stopped as soon as she realized we were all listening.

Mom leaned over the low dividing wall from the kitchen to shush her. "This has nothing to do with him. Brian's been dead since the early fifties."

But... hadn't Bee's letter to me said that she had been known as Brian before her "change of life?" And what could she have abandoned that caused her death sixty years later?

If Bee had had a stalker from sixty years ago, it was a long-lived one. Whether it was love or hate, sixty years is a long time to hold onto it. My entire lifetime, in fact.

"Is the stalker something new, or did she always have one?" asked Ben. Trust him to cut to the heart of the matter like a hot knife through butter.

"Don't rightly know," said Burt. "Bee wasn't one to complain or talk about her problems." He sounded proud, as if bottling everything up had made one strong.

I couldn't help thinking if she had been killed by someone she knew, telling others about their issues might have saved her. Sorrow is a heavy, physical weight.

EVENTUALLY, I WAS ALONE with Luci, Ben, and Miko. I'd been mainlining a strong black tea for the past two hours and was now jittery and exhausted, instead of just exhausted. Pardon me, but it didn't seem like an improvement.

"Vee, did your aunt ever mention having trouble with her neighbors? Or seeing a stranger over and over again?" Miko asked me.

"Just ask if I knew her stalker. Or if I suspect anyone. Stop being coy."

A line formed between his well-groomed eyebrows, and he opened his mouth to say something when Victor practically exploded.

He dove off of my lap, leaving angry red welts I could feel, and raced for the front door, barking and growling.

He'd never done that before. I mean, he'd growled at people who were angry or rough with me, but not like this. To hear him, you'd think he was a Rottweiler.

I hurried to the front door, calling for Victor to calm down, but once I arrived, I was nervous to open it. So, I peered through the curtained window and saw... nothing. Not even a squirrel.

Miko gently pushed me to one side, and with one hand on his gun, threw the door open. I hadn't even noticed him following me.

Victor bolted out the door, still in a barking frenzy. He tore through the hedge and I could hear his barking moving across the neighbor's yard.

Miko and I burst through my door together, and I ignored his commands to stay in the house. After all, this was *my* dog racing toward danger. Or a squirrel. Maybe a cat.

But my hip hurt too much to run, so Miko lost me as he raced around the hedge, following my stalwart but tiny protector.

Ben came up to me and slipped a sweater over my shoulders.

"If you sit on the porch, I'll catch up with Miko and see what's going on. I'll call you so you don't even have to wait." He met my eye steadily, and I nodded. I didn't want to fall again, and my leg was shaky.

As soon as I'd agreed, Ben loped off to the road and followed the faint sound of barking and yipping.

I turned to go sit on the porch chair and nearly fell over. I felt the blood drain from my face as my ears started to ring.

Someone had painted "Your Next" in red on my door. I thought, *My next what?* as I slowly sat on the grass.

A shiver worked its way up my spine, and I shuddered. I needed tea. No, I'd had too much already. I needed a sweater. I already had the one Ben brought me.

I was still sitting on the grass when Ben came back. My mind had wandered a little bit, and his voice startled me.

"Oh, my Lord, Vee, where did that come from?"

I turned to see him staring open-mouthed at my door. I hadn't imagined it, then.

"I don't know. I haven't done anything. Why would someone write this?" I sounded weak. I hated seeming weak, so I gestured for Ben to help me up.

We moved closer to the door, arm in arm. And I'm not sure who was holding whom up, or which one of us needed the comfort more. The red paint—and I was praying it was paint—had dripped from the letters, leaving streaks down my bright blue door. It had even splashed a little onto the butter yellow trim. The whole thing would need repainting.

"I need to call Miko," said Ben, but he didn't reach for his phone. He just stood, staring. "They must have done this while we were inside. What if they'd been dangerous?"

"Miko would have handled it," I said. A thought wormed its way into the front of my mind. "This must be who Victor is chasing. What if they hurt him?"

Ben shook his head. "Not with Miko hot on their trail."

He carefully opened the door and we edged in, trying not to smear the paint.

The parlor was a disheveled mess, and two of the dining room chairs were still in there. I couldn't face cleaning up. I felt too exhausted, too scared, and too worried about Victor.

But there weren't any options, so I started collecting dishes and headed for the kitchen.

Ben followed a couple of minutes later, several cups and saucers balanced in his hands.

"Do you want me to move all the chairs back where they go?"

"No, I'll do it later." I said in a voice that fooled no-one. Ben shook his head and headed back out of the room. Seconds later I heard the scrape of a chair leg on my wooden floor. I'd have cringed if I'd had the energy.

Exhaustion swept over me like a tidal wave, and I swayed on my feet. Seems the fright I'd had had burned the jitters right out of me, I could've fallen asleep leaning against the sink.

I shuffled to the living room to help Ben, but it was mostly done. I settled onto the sofa and promptly fell asleep.

Chapter Six

I woke from a dream about Victor leaving bloody footprints wherever he went.

Miko and Ben had been whispering by the stairs going up to the bedrooms. Well, Ben had been whispering. Miko had just said my name, which I suppose was what interrupted my dream of cleaning up endless paw prints.

Miko asked about the door, but I had no answers for him—he was on his own. My head felt muzzy from the interrupted nap and my temper short from too much caffeine. I felt bad about it, even as I heard myself snark at him.

Miko's expressive eyes looked disappointed; I'd apologize later. Right now, I needed a nap. And my dog.

"Where's Victor?" I was barely aware of cutting Ben off mid-sentence as Victor's absence became clear.

Miko turned pink. "I lost him. Them. I'm sorry, but I'm sure he'll turn up. Dogs are good at backtracking like that."

Fear woke me all the way up. Woke my temper, too.

Next thing you knew, we were all out searching, including a poor constable Miko had called on his cell.

We found Victor safe and happy at the park across the street to Watson Lane. He had been chasing ducks bigger than he was.

I guess he lost the perp, too. I didn't care; I just wanted to go home and take a nap before bedtime. Or maybe just have an early bedtime. There were lots of leftovers for supper.

I wouldn't even need a martini to get to sleep.

MONDAY DAWNED WAY TOO early.

The sky was overcast but not raining, and I still felt sore and grumpy from yesterday. But there was no point to staying in bed all day even if I was short on spoons. I decided to forgo a shower in favor of a quick wash, to save energy.

Victor seemed quieter than usual, too. I guess the ducks had worn him out.

Breakfast consisted of a couple of frozen waffles—I warned you I wasn't much for cooking—and a large mug of coffee. It didn't sit right in my stomach, so I decided to look into something that had been bothering me.

Was "Bee's Brian" the same Brian that died in 1953? Where had she been living? Had there been a stalker back then? I kind of hoped so; a ninety-year-old stalker should be safe enough to deal with.

The Smiths Falls library was in a lovely, century-old brick building. They'd turned the tower windows on all three floors into seating and kept the Victorian vibe throughout the building. It had been my favourite place when I was young. I hadn't considered how much I dreaded seeing it all updated and modernized until my chest relaxed. I'd been holding my breath.

But the smell of furniture wax and old books was better than drugs for relaxing all my tight muscles. I took a deep breath and smiled at the woman behind the big checkout desk.

I hurried away, not wanting help, not wanting to share this trip into the past in search of Bee's secrets. It seemed rude to bring someone else in.

But forty minutes later, I'd given up. I'd searched all three floors and tried to get into the attic. I could not find the microfiche section for the life of me. I couldn't even find the stairs to the basement where it had been. Well, I thought I found the stairs, but the door was locked with a big "no admittance to the public" sign bolted to it.

So, I took the elevator from the third floor back to the ground floor. The one modern convenience I felt happy about.

The woman at the desk had been replaced by a teenager with spiky, pink hair. Really pink, almost fuchsia. Not that it was any of my business.

In truth, I was a bit jealous. I could never dye my hair a wild colour at my age, and proud as I was to still be mostly brown instead of grey, I wanted to see what I'd look like in bold purple.

I grinned, remembering a librarian at my high school who'd used a purply-blue rinse in her white hair. If my hair ever went all white, I might do that. Or maybe a pastel colour. I'd seen that in a magazine.

"Hello, Miss!"

I startled, realizing I'd been standing and staring at the girl for a few minutes. She looked a bit ticked off, and her tone had lost its practiced politeness as she'd tried to get my attention.

"Oh, I am sorry, I just wondered how I'd look in your hair. Colour. In your hair colour. Pink." I could feel the blood rising in my cheeks.

She stared at me for a moment, then grinned. "I think it might be a bit bright for your skin tones. You're more peachy than pinky in your face."

"I hadn't thought of that. What would go with peach? Green?" I made a bit of a face at that thought, I liked green well enough but not for my hair.

"Oh, you could still do pink if you liked, just not a strong, blue-based pink like this." She tilted her head and squinted a little. "A rosy-peach would definitely work, but so would a pastel pink, if you wanted just pink."

She laughed. "I haven't said the word pink so many times in one conversation since I was four."

I laughed with her. Then I waved my hand to brush away the question of hair colour.

"I actually came in to find some newspapers from the early fifties, preferably local ones. I can't find the microfiche machines anywhere."

She laughed again. I thought teenagers were supposed to be sullen.

"We got rid of those years ago. Everything's on computer now."

"Even those old things? I mean, I want just the local papers. Not Toronto."

"Oh, yeah. Scanning everything into a database was a grad project a few years ago. It's not searchable, though." She frowned a little, and I suspected she was thinking I was too old to understand her.

"That's all right. I was prepared to do a day-by-day search anyway. Maybe you can suggest to the high school that they make improving the database this year's grad project."

"That's not a bad idea. And working here would give me credibility." She waved to someone behind me. "Thanks!"

I'd been dismissed.

BY THE TIME I GOT HOME, I was starving. It was just after one, but those waffles had been long since gone. I'd considered stopping for lunch at the Bun Journee, but I was still peopled-out from the weekend, and Ben would probably have wanted to talk.

Luci still stayed at my place. She'd planned to leave, but one look at my front door, and she'd set down roots like a Sequoia.

She must have spent the morning cleaning my front door, and a weight lifted from my spirit to see only a few reddish smudges still there. I hoped the police had done everything yesterday.

"Hello, Luci? You still here?" There was silence. No Victor either, so I headed out back.

Sure enough, they were in the garden. Well, Luci was in the garden. Victor danced around, chasing the birds that flew over the yard. As soon as the screen door thunked shut behind me, Luci turned and smiled.

Getting to her feet, she wiped dirt from her knees and pushed her hair back behind her ears. This left dirt smudges on her cheeks, making her look a bit like a garden elf. The brown suede jeans, tucked into her knee-high boots and topped with a turtle-neck sweater, didn't do much to dispel the illusion.

I grinned just looking at her. When she picked up a big salad bowl filled with the last of the onions, tomatoes and peppers, my grin grew wider.

I had been stalling on putting the garden to bed because I'd been afraid kneeling on the cold dirt would hurt. Now I didn't have to!

Over a quick lunch made of leftover cooked chicken and fried tomatoes and onions with frozen vegetables all over microwaved rice, I filled Luci in on my search at the library.

She chewed thoughtfully as I talked, seemingly concerned by my meagre findings. But let's face it; my dad's family weren't movers and shakers, so they didn't make the papers often.

And what I had found didn't really help.

Brian had married Margaret Turnbull in June of 1950. There was a birth announcement of a girl eight months later. They named the girl Mary-Elizabeth.

Then his obituary was published in 1953, where it was noted that he left behind a wife, a daughter, and an infant son. Also, his parents had died in a car accident a few months before. I hadn't found either their accident or obituaries, but several weeks were missing from the database. The library had probably lost the newspapers before the high school kids could scan them.

His obituary also said that he drowned while on a fishing trip, and the body hadn't been recovered. That gave me an itch to learn more. *I watch way too many mystery movies. No body equals not dead. Maybe.*

AFTER TIDYING UP THE kitchen, I decided to go back to the library to do a further search of my family history. This time, I was not only going to hold myself to only Brian, but I was also going to search for the whole fam-damily.

Smiths Falls is really a pretty place. Most of the buildings are mid-Victorian brick with lovely white ginger-breading around the eaves and wraparound porches. Even the more modern houses had been built to fit in, so they had porches with roofs and columns.

The park at the end of my street straddled the Rideau River and included a small island you could get to by a wrought-iron bridge. Since the library was right downtown, I could either take a bus at the end of the street and go around the park, or I could take a nice long walk through the park and end up only a block away from the library. Victor voted for the walk.

The weather was cool but already warmer than it had been, so I dressed my wee puppy in layers. He looked so adorable in a hooded sweatshirt with a little denim jacket over it, and the hood pulled out to lie along his back.

It really was a lovely time of day for a walk. The sun warmed my back, and the streets were not too crowded. I nodded to a few people here and there, but mostly strolled alone as I pushed my walker down to the river and over the bridge. Victor and I had a disagreement about comportment once we reached the island, though.

He thought the casual denim jacket meant that he was free to run around chasing birds, ducks, and digging through the underbrush. I disagreed. We all know who won that fight.

While I sat on a bench, waiting, I thought through what I wanted to look up and wrote it down on the back of an envelope. My mom said that Brian had died in the early fifties, and I knew that Aunt Bee had moved back to Smiths Falls in 1953. My earlier research shows that Brian had left behind a wife and two kids. What happened to them? Bee's daughter would be my age, or a bit older. No one had mentioned seeing some old biddy hanging around, so I wrote her off as a suspect.

I remembered the Wedgwood blue car that honked at me. But the glimpse I had gotten of the driver was not an old man, well, old is relative. I'm a very young 60, while I imagined the abandoned little boy to be a very old 60.

Vanity, thy name is Victoria.

I realized that I hadn't seen or heard Victor for a while. As I stood up to go look for him, I saw my fickle, furless friend trotting along at the feet of a teenage girl who approached me. Her hands were in the pockets of her denim jacket, and if Victor had been wearing torn jeans, they would have made a nice couple.

"Hello, thank you for finding Victor. I was just about to go looking for him." I smiled at the girl who seemed very familiar. Where could I have seen her before? "Do you work at the Timmy's just up street from Watson Lane?"

"No, why the fark would I work there? Is this your weird-looking dog?"

Her attitude proved that she didn't work in any of the nice, upscale stores I'd been shopping in recently. In fact, even fast food wouldn't hire her with that mouth.

"My boy is not weird-looking, he has a skin condition." I patted my leg and Victor trotted over, though he did try to squirm away when I bent over to reattach his leash. The girl shook her head.

"Lady, that is the weirdest looking dog I've ever seen. I'm not even sure it's a dog."

She was not endearing herself to me. Her familiarity itched my brain in a place I couldn't scratch. Where had I seen her before? She wasn't the girl who worked at the library. For one thing, her hair was blue and not pink.

"I'm Victoria Lilley. What's your name?" I smiled. Her name might give me a clue as to where I'd seen her. Was she one of Burt's grandkids?

But she did not give me her name, she just glowered at me. On the other hand, she didn't leave. I decide outwait her. After what seemed several minutes of just staring at each other, she shook her head and a wry grin split her face.

"I know who you are. I just don't know how we're related."

I could feel my mouth fall open and scrambled for something to say, so it would look like I intended to open my mouth.

"We're related?" That wasn't the wittiest thing I could have come up with, but it was all I could think of. She was about the same age as the girl in the library, far too young to be one of my sister Karey's kids, even if she had a girl. Which she didn't. Her strange hair colour skewed her age; she might have been one of my nephew's kids. Her attitude seemed similar, but I hoped neither of the boys had ever bred. And although I didn't know all of Aunt Kay's grandchildren, I was pretty sure Blue Hair wasn't one of them.

"Yeah, your uncle Brian was my great-grandfather. I just don't know his relationship with Beatrice or your mother."

I was still standing there with my mouth hanging open, when a familiar man ran up and grabbed her by the elbow. Unless I was very much mistaken, which I rarely am, it was the driver of the Wedgwood blue car. But they were both too young to be Aunt Bee's stalker.

"Brian was my mom's brother-in-law, my dad's brother," I said. Why was I telling them this? There was no proof they were who she said they were. But somehow, I believed her. I wasn't telling her a thing about Aunt Bee, though.

"Margaret! How many times have I told you to stay away from her?" The man shook her by the arm. She cut her eyes at him, then stuck out her tongue.

"I'm 18 years old, I'm not a kid. I can make my own decisions."

Well, I didn't like physical violence of any kind, even if the little brat did deserve it. I stepped into the middle of their argument to distract him.

"Hello? Let me know if I'm out of line, but who the fudge crackle are you two? And why have you been driving past my house so often?" I crossed my arms and glared at them. I'm sure that I looked regal and slightly intimidating. Until Victor whined and jumped up, putting muddy paw-prints all over my pale blue jeans. I don't know where he'd been when the girl found him, but I was not picking him up. Not until his paws were cleaner.

"Oh, I haven't been driving past your place, I mean, I don't know where you live."

I shot him my most disbelieving expression. "But you told her to stay away from me?"

He glanced at the girl, and she started laughing.

"Oh, that's great, Dad, yell at me for talking to her and then lie in the most unconvincing way ever."

"Look you two, I know you," I said, pointing at the man, "have been driving past my place and staring at me. And you," I turned my finger to point at the girl, "are probably the one making me feel like someone is staring at the back of my neck all the time. I have a very sensitive neck."

That wasn't exactly what I'd meant to say, but I hadn't exactly seen her before, although I had certainly felt like I was being watched. I figured the odds were good this was her doing. And the look on her face confirmed it. I practically shouted, *"AHA!"*

Their eyes met, then the man looked at his feet. He shuffled a bit, more like a two year old than a 42 year old.

"Didn't realize you'd seen me," he said.

The girl shook her head again, this time rolling her eyes into the bargain. The man moved his gaze from her to me and then started laughing ruefully. "Okay, you caught me. Could I buy you a cup of coffee? This will take some explaining."

I wasn't entirely sure of his motives, but he seemed to have an open and honest face. I found myself agreeing before I'd actually weighed any of the cons. But I made sure to lead him to the Bun Journee—I was going to have backup no matter what.

WE WALKED THROUGH THE door and were enveloped by the intoxicating scent of cinnamon, vanilla, and coffee. My hip was also really grateful for the warmth of the slightly overfull room. I hadn't realized how far the walk was to downtown and as usual, my hip let me know in no uncertain terms that it wasn't pleased.

I caught Ben's eye as he bent to place more baked goods in the glass front, and a big, dimpled grin broke out on his face. I realized this was probably the first time I'd seen him in weeks for just a social call—not that this was merely a social call.

But it sure felt good to see him.

Ben waved the waitress off and hurried over to show us to our table, the only empty one in the shop. He gave me a hug and a French air-kiss beside each cheek; I could feel my face heat up a little. I turned to introduce him to the others and realized I had no idea who they were.

"Oh Ben, this is..." I stared pointedly at the man who blushed. How rare to see a man who blushes, especially at his age. It was too cute.

"I am, um, Mark Lilley, and this is my daughter Margaret."

Ben's eyes got round, and he looked from the man to me a couple of times before stuttering, "Lilley? Are you and Vee related?"

I raised my eyebrows at Mark as if to say, "Well, are we?" Margaret started laughing again. I was getting quite peeved with what she found amusing.

"I think we need a cup of coffee first; it will be easier to explain over coffee." Mark made a stern gesture at his daughter, who totally ignored him.

"Three coffees coming up." Ben gave me a very speaking look before he headed back to the counter. I could tell he meant to find out what was going on. Not that I could blame them, if I were him I'd be dying of curiosity, too. Well, actually, even as myself, I was dying of curiosity.

As expected, Ben pulled over a chair and with the fourth coffee in hand, he sat with us. I was grateful for his silent support as Mark started talking, interrupted frequently by Margaret.

"My father's name was Mitchell, my grandfather was Brian Lilley. I only found that out when my dad died last year. I mean, I knew my grandfather's name but all I knew was that he had gone fishing and drowned when my father was just a baby." Mark paused to take a drink of his coffee.

Margaret jumped into the pause in the conversation. "It turned out that my grandfather had been doing some research on his father's death, and on his family. Of course, by the time he began investigating, his parents were dead, but he did find his father's marriage certificate, and that led him to Smiths Falls." Margaret glanced at her father and grinned, "You were moving too slow."

I had a sinking suspicion I knew the answer, but I had to ask. "Just what does this have to do with me? There's a whole family tree of Lilleys here."

Mark had the grace to seem embarrassed, but Margaret just pressed on excitedly. "I had a friend sort of hack the bank, the one where my great-grandfather had a bank account when he died."

"What?! Margaret, you hacked a bank! Are you crazy?" cried Mark. "Have you any idea how illegal that is?"

Margaret rolled her eyes. "I didn't hack it. I had Josephine hack it. She's way good."

Mark looked like he wanted to bang his head on the table, or maybe hers.

"I still don't see what that has to do with me," I said, not wanting them to stop talking. They seemed to have the answers I lacked, and I might have the answers they sought.

"Ugh, don't you people get it?" Margaret glared back and forth between me and her father. "Someone had taken $2000 out of the account two days before he disappeared. The cops assumed that was to pay for his fishing trip, but seriously, in 1953 it cost $2000? That sounds like running-away money to me."

She was right, I had to admit. In 1953, going fishing probably cost 50 bucks. Including the boat and cabin rental. So, Brian had run back to Smiths Falls. I guess Bee's letter had been right. I ought to have felt better having that mystery solved, but it didn't seem in keeping with Bee's character to empty the bank account before running out on her wife and kids.

I needed space to think about that, and maybe talk to Mom and Aunt Kay. But now that Mark had found me, they seemed to have a million questions.

"We are not sure how you fit into this, but we're pretty sure that Beatrice Lilley was Brian Lilley's second wife." Mark cradled his coffee cup in his hands and stared into its empty depths.

"And Dad really means second wife, since Brian had already had one." Margaret smirked, and my hand itched to smack her. Why are know-it-all teenagers so annoying? Oh yeah, they think that older people know nothing. Not that I considered myself an older person, just older than her.

I didn't want to explain to them how Bee and Brian were related; it seemed too much like breaking Bee's confidence. There was also the question of how these two were related to me; I mean, I know how they were related to me now. They were cousins because Kay and Bee were my dad's siblings. But they didn't even know of my existence before they got here.

I had a dreadful thought.

Were they Bee's legal heirs, regardless of what her will said? If Mark's grandfather really was Brian, and then Brian had "become" Bee, then wasn't Mark her obvious heir? Could he have the will overturned? I wondered if Bee had kept tabs on her old family. I sure hoped not, since that would mean she deliberately left them in the cold.

Mark and I sat there, lost in our own thoughts, while Margaret stared around the room at the people like they were a zoo exhibit. Finally, she puffed her cheeks out and blew a disgusted sigh across the table. Mark shook his head at her; Margaret just rolled her eyes again and slowly lowered her forehead to the table.

I smiled to myself. Regardless of whether they knew about Bee or not, they were family. They seemed accepting of me, and I needed all the accepting family I could find. I wondered how my mother would take knowing about them.

I turned to wave at Ben to get more coffee and was just in time to see Burt walk through the door. His eyes lit up when he saw me, then he frowned a little upon noticing Mark and Margaret. Still, he headed straight for us and Ben's empty chair.

"Excuse me, we're having a private conversation here," said Margaret. She glared at Burt. Then Mark glared at Margaret, and Burt glared back at both of them.

"Ganging up on my Vee, are you? Seems to me I'm just here to even things out." Burt waved at the waitress before returning his frown to Mark. I reached over to lay my hand on top of his and felt his fist relax a little.

"Burt, I'd like you to meet my cousin Mark and his daughter Margaret," I said. "We're just getting to know each other."

Mark's eyebrows raced for his hairline before a slow smile spread across his face. Margaret just froze for a moment, then smirked again.

I swear by every ice cream flavor I know, I'm going to slap that girl. Well, not really, since I didn't believe in that, but she sure was getting under my skin. Had I been that way as a teenager? Sudden sympathy for my mom surged in my heart.

I never did make it to the library. But after too much coffee and too few real details, Mark said he and Margaret had better get home. They lived out the other side of Perth, about 40 minutes away. I could see it was just an excuse; they had as much thinking to do as I did.

Burt offered me a lift home, which I would have refused because I needed time to think, but when I tried to stand up, I knew I had better take it. Sitting for two hours after all that walking had left my hip a wee bit unhappy.

Not as unhappy as Victor, though, who still sulked at not being allowed on my lap with his muddy feet. I don't know why he was upset; Ben had brought him a little bowl of milk and a scrambled egg. He should have been feeling spoiled.

Once home, I pulled off Victor's muddy clothes and carried him to the bathroom to wash him in the sink. It's a good thing he was so small. It was also a good thing he enjoyed splashing in puddles since that meant he had a good time in the warm water and bubbles.

I needed to talk to someone. Not Burt, someone who would listen to my worries about Bee. I wasn't sure where the girls were and didn't want to talk to Helen. Who did that leave?

I reminded myself that Mom and I had been getting along a lot better, and I sat down in front of my computer to call her on that Skype thingy. Of course, she didn't answer.

I was completely coffeed out but still wanted something to drink, if only to keep my hands busy. I thought, *Fudge that,* then made up a pitcher of martinis and put it in the fridge. I figured by the time it was cold, I would know who I needed to talk to. Still feeling restless, I went into the kitchen and started chopping random vegetables. Maybe Luci could figure out something to make from them for supper.

I created several neat piles of colorful veggies but it didn't calm me down. I looked around the kitchen. The girls had washed and put away the dishes, the floor was clean, and through the patio door I could see that the deck had been tidied up of newspapers and empty plastic cups.

Black Sesame ice cream! I needed something to do, or I would do something unwise, like phone Mark and tell him everything. For some reason, I didn't want him to know about Aunt Bee's connection to the "uncle" Mark sought.

I didn't think I was being greedy about the money, although the money had been very nice. It was more that their existence brought up a huge character flaw in my previously flawless aunt. If Mark had birth certificates to prove who they were, I really would have to talk to my lawyer.

I knew I would need to share some of the money with them. Bee had wanted me to have all of it, but logically, it should've gone to them. And, if I was being honest, I thought they deserved to have it.

There was no help for it; I had to speak to the estate lawyer.

But at least I knew who they were, probably not Bee's stalkers, and not the people who had been threatening me.

Maybe. *I mean, why would they? Unless they were lying about not knowing who Aunt Bee was and were trying to scare me into giving up my inheritance.*

But the tiniest bit of me was overjoyed to have more family.

Chapter Seven

Victor whined and tried to back up when I opened the front door. He was wearing a sweet argyle sweater in blue and green with bright pink lines over the green diamonds. His green fleece-lined rain-boots almost matched his sweater. *What can you do? I tried.*

But warm as his sweater was, he did not want to go out. It was strange; he usually leaped out the door like his butt was on fire. But after tugging at his leash for several seconds while he dug his paws into the step, I gave up. I didn't even bother taking his sweater off, I just unclipped his leash and let him run back into the house.

Luci and I had dressed warmly to go to Helen's for supper. It might only have been four doors down; however, not only had a chill wind sprung up, but it was also trying to rain. Damp, cold, windy, bleh! I hated this type of fall weather. Where were my gorgeous orange and red leaves?

Helen had been oddly insistent when she'd called this afternoon. I felt sore and tired from my morning at the park, and just wanted to veg in front of the television. But here I was, missing my show and limping along the uneven sidewalk.

The sisters' home was a mirror image to mine. The bay window was on the right instead of the left side of the front door. That likely meant that the kitchen-dining room combination were on the left, and I wondered if the bathroom was still tucked behind the living room. Most of these old war houses were the same, built for returning soldiers by the government, following World War II. They used only two or three blueprints across the whole country. Single story and small, with either two or three bedrooms. The basements had cement walls and floors, so you could put in more space if you wanted to. Bee hadn't done this, but Greta had.

Since the basement door was even with the driveway and the main floor had a few stairs to get to it, we'd come in the lower level. Greta had built herself a small apartment, one bedroom, a kitchenette and a living room. It had been decorated in shades of cream and brown. Not to my taste, but cozy with knitted blankets on the furniture and an electric fireplace in the living room.

She hustled us straight to the stairs, and I groaned. We should've just used the front door instead because that option only presented a half-dozen steps.

By the time we got upstairs from the basement; I huffed and puffed like a broken steam engine. Luci had cupped her hands under my butt to give me subtle but very helpful pushes up the stairs.

The scent hit me as soon as I opened the door to the main floor. Roast chicken, a comfort food from my childhood. My belly growled loudly enough to be heard behind me. Luci giggled.

"Oh, come in, come in." Helen grinned, waving at us with oven mitts still on her hands. She turned and headed back into the kitchen from the short hall. I pulled off my boots and followed her in stocking feet. Luci had to half-sit, half-lean against the wall to untie hers. I should have warned her, but my mind was on other things.

Like, why wasn't I at home drinking a martini?

Turned out that the dinner would be less about Luci and me, and more about my aunt. It also became clear that Greta had a Bee in her bonnet. *Ha!*

Bee had mentioned to Helen that she had been getting small gifts left in her mailbox or at her door for years, with no idea who had left them.

She'd been anxious early on, but after a couple of years, she'd seemed pretty accepting of them.

"In fact," Helen leaned in to whisper, "She'd been flattered. Not many people get a secret admirer that lasts for that long."

Greta disagreed. "Just because they didn't kill her right away doesn't mean they didn't kill her. Maybe they finally got tired of waiting for her to love them back."

Helen shook her head, frowning at her sister. "Nonsense. The letters were too sweet for a deranged killer to have written them."

Greta grunted, looking at me strangely. "It was probably Burt."

I took a sip of the sweet German wine they'd served with dinner, then asked, "The killer or the secret admirer? Because he hasn't been too secret about his crush on Aunt Bee or that he left her anonymous notes." I paused and sipped again. "Just disappointed."

Luci placed her napkin onto her empty plate and smiled at Greta. Normally Lucia's smile could melt stone. Greta was made of sterner stuff.

She scowled. "I suppose you think you knew her just because you drove down from Ottawa a couple times a year. Well, we were neighbors for over twenty years, and I can tell you, Bee wasn't what she seemed. In fact—" and she stared pointedly at Helen, "There was a woman visiting her the last few months. Long visits, if you know what I mean."

With that, Greta got up and headed for the kitchen with Luci's plate. Luci met my eyes and raised her eyebrows. I knew exactly what she meant: *Who was this woman? I pointed at Luci and mouthed Jaqi.*

From the kitchen, I heard Greta still snarling over Bee. "Everybody thought she was such an angel, wouldn't say shit if her mouth was full of it... no saint, believe you me!"

Helen smiled apologetically as we heard the basement door slam shut. "Greta's been upset since Bee died; she just hates to show it."

We all agreed that she just missed her friend, although I didn't see it.

I didn't see it at all.

After dinner, Helen wanted to play a board game. She looked so sad when I tried to refuse that I felt guilty for wanting to go home. I discreetly popped a couple of my pain pills and managed to be gracious. Barely.

Helen had called Greta back upstairs because the game worked best with four players. It was surprisingly fun, yet not so involved that we couldn't chat while playing. It combined cards, dice, and a board with little plastic men. I peered closer at mine. People. Maybe mannequins. Definitely eunuchs.

Greta got grumpier the longer we played, and when I won my third game in a row, she practically melted down.

"Helen, I don't know why you insist on playing this awful game. No one likes it but you."

"Bee loved it," Helen replied softly.

"Well, Bee isn't here." Greta stomped out of the room, headed toward the alcove by the kitchen where her stairs were. "And these two are barely putting up with you."

The door to her downstairs apartment slammed shut.

We were all silent for a moment. I'd never imagined such a stolid woman could be such a bad loser.

Luci reached across the table to grasp Helen's hand. "We are so not putting you up." She looked over at me for confirmation. "We are having fun, and you are telling us stories."

Helen smiled sadly. "I wouldn't want to keep you if you want to go." She reached for the box the game came in, and I pulled it out of her reach.

"If Luci doesn't mind going to let Victor out for a widdle, we're happy to keep playing. I should give you a chance to win back your pennies, after all." I looked at Luci to see if she was okay with being volunteered, and she nodded.

Helen looked relieved, "You could bring him back with you, dear. I love little dogs."

Luci headed to the back hall to get her coat and shoes but left via the front door.

Helen looked pensive, so I lumbered to my feet to make more tea and search for a snack. Every house had a stash of cookies somewhere.

Luci hadn't returned by the time I brought the tea back to the living room. I poured us each a cup, leaving Luci's empty for the time being.

Helen smiled and nodded as she grabbed a couple of the cookies I'd found in the cupboard over the fridge. They were maple cream.

"These were your aunt's favorites, you know. I always kept some on hand for her." Helen's eyes shone with sudden tears. "I miss her so much. So much more than Gertie does."

I reached for her hand, but she moved it away. Odd.

"We spent a lot of time together. It still doesn't feel real that she's gone." She wiped at her eyes. Forcing a not-so-believable smile, Helen started to reset the board for another game. "I often thought how much nicer it would be if she lived with me and Greta lived alone. Of course, Greta would never go for that. If only to keep me from being happy."

I thought about that. Bee had loved living on her own. She'd often mentioned how she enjoyed being able to eat when she wanted or wear her robe all day. Still, I saw Helen's point about her sister.

A brief knock sounded at the door before it opened, and Victor raced in. His tail wagged so hard as he bounced in front of Helen that his whole bottom wiggled. Helen laughed and bent over for doggie kisses.

I was about to ask about Greta's attitude when I realized that Luci remained standing by the front door.

"Is something wrong, sweetie?" I turned to see her better. Her freckles were standing out on her too-pale skin.

But she glanced at Helen and shook her head.

While Victor kept Helen distracted, I walked up to Luci.

"Spill it." I lowered my brows from their puzzled position near my hairline, but Luci just shook her head again.

"I don't want... We need to go home," Luci whispered at me while pointing her jaw at Helen. And of course, Helen had heard her and looked up. I could see the instant she noticed Luci's pallor by her expression.

"Oh, my dear girl, what's the matter?" Helen softly pushed Victor away and hurried over to us.

"Victor was outside." Luci's voice wavered a bit as she gazed into my eyes. "Someone was there. In the house."

I gripped her hand, pulling her stark stare away from my face where it was getting uncomfortable. I could feel my knuckles go white, and she pulled at her hand to loosen my grip.

"Why do you think someone was in the house?" I heard my heart pick up speed.

"I saw a light on the wall in the kitchen."

I shook my head. I'd left the light over the stove on in case we were late getting back. "Oh, Luci. It's just the fan."

"No, Vee, the light moved when I opened the door, like it was going into the hallway."

"Oh." I looked at Helen, who looked back at Luci. We had to check it out.

MY FRONT DOOR HUNG open. With all of the lights off inside, the house seemed like it had been abandoned. We stood in a huddle at the end of the driveway: me, Luci, and Helen. I held Victor, and even he was quiet and still.

I glanced at Luci and she shrugged, moving a step closer to the house.

"There was a light. I swear it." Though she didn't sound so sure about it now.

Well, the house wasn't getting any emptier, and we weren't getting any warmer huddling in the dead leaves and wind.

I started up the driveway, trying to hear past the silence. Was there a rustle in the hedge? Was that a reflection from the moon in my bedroom window or a flashlight?

I muttered, "The hell with it," and pulled out my cellphone. "We have cops who can deal with this."

The voice at the other end of the 9-1-1 call sounded bored, which didn't help my mood. It's far easier to be angry than terrified, so I got mad at him.

"I'm not going inside to check the house. That's why I'm calling you." I gestured angrily in the direction of the house just as the light in my bedroom went out. "Shit a brick and hit me with it!"

"I—what? What happened?" The voice on the phone sounded tiny as my hand moved it away from my ear without permission. A small light appeared in the hall.

I yelled into my cell, no doubt deafening the poor man on the other end.

"There's someone with a flashlight in there!"

Luci took my yelp as an instruction to race into the house to catch the intruder, the 9-1-1 operator shouted at me to stay out of the house, and Helen...

Well, Helen dithered. She walked a step or two toward the door, then back to me. I dropped Victor, who was squirming to get down, and he shot off after Luci.

He might fit in my purse, but he had the heart of a lion. I calmly told the operator we were following Luci into the house. He said to stay put and wait, but I was never good at that obedience thing. Especially when Luci might be in danger.

Victor disappeared through the front door, still barking. I hurried as fast as I could through the darkened grass. My porch light was off.

A cold breeze blew past my neck, and I shivered. I knew I was better off staying put and was about to tell Helen as much when Victor stopped barking.

I ran for the door. Halfway there, I heard Luci scream.

Next thing I knew, I was standing in my bedroom doorway staring at Luci holding a bloodied puppy in her hands. My vision swam a little, and I heard Helen gasp behind me.

"It's a toy," Luci whispered. "It's just a toy."

I reached over and took it from her. It was a toy. A toy Chihuahua. It was pretty lifelike except for being half the size of Victor.

It had been slit up the belly and the packed Styrofoam beads were spilling over my fingers like white blood.

Red ink or paint had been smeared around the cut to look like blood. It bore an uncanny resemblance to Victor. I felt a little faint and woozy, even as I registered Constable Smith's voice and footsteps downstairs.

"Up here," I whispered. Helen cleared her throat, then shouted down for the cops to come up.

Which they did. Loudly. I also heard Greta yelling at them, and us I assumed, to ask what was going on and why were we over here.

If Ben showed up, I'd need to put the tea on. *Hey, hey, the gang's all here.*

Luci pushed me down onto the edge of the bed and shoved my head between my knees. I didn't know why I was cuddling the destroyed toy and crying, when Victor was at my feet begging to be picked up.

I just held the toy and tried to breathe deeply, which wasn't happening in this position. I could hear Greta berating Helen for the fuss. I wanted to kick her in her sturdy shins but couldn't from where I was.

The last thing I heard before fainting was Burt demanding to know what was going on and MacGuinty telling him to go home.

THE SUN PEEKED CHEERILY around the edge of my bedroom curtains, framing the snapshots of Bee and me on the wall, and burning my eyeballs like fireplace poker.

I didn't care what clock said; it was too early. The cops hadn't left until after 2:00 a.m. Then the sisters had stayed to argue over the danger and whether Luci, the still-alive Chihuahua, and I were welcome to stay at their house.

I heard far more about who owned the house and why they were living together than I'd ever wanted to. It's true what they say about two women in one kitchen. Just don't. Ever. Not even sisters.

Oh, it had worked for Jaqi, Luci, and me but that's because we all knew it was Luci's kitchen. And there wasn't room to have anyone else stay over, so that argument had never come up.

The sun didn't go away when I told it to, so I dragged my tired carcass to the ensuite shower. I'd been dubious about the loss of a third bedroom when Bee had had the ensuite built, but I was grateful now that she'd ignored me.

I knew Luci was around somewhere, no doubt looking fresh as a Sunday morning, so I ignored the noises coming from downstairs.

I struggled, just the teeniest bit, to pull a lacy camisole over my shoulders when I heard footsteps coming up the stairs. Heavy ones, definitely not Lucia.

I tugged harder and felt the silky fabric rip as it cleared my linebacker shoulders and slid into place.

My door was flung wide and Burt stood there, red faced and scowling. I yanked the sheet to cover my mostly undressed dignity.

Burt paused and appeared to notice me for the first time.

We stared at each other as red slowly crept up both our faces. Burt spoke first.

"Where's—I was expecting—I'm sorry." He turned his head but not before a strange expression crossed his face. Equal parts confusion, disappointment and... anger? He shuffled back into the hall and quietly pulled the door closed behind him.

How odd.

I got dressed quickly and hurried downstairs.

Luci stood in the hallway glaring at Burt, who hung his head, looking for all the world like a puppy caught misbehaving.

"I don't know what I was thinking. I saw that man leaving so late... I don't know what I thought."

Luci stared at his face through lowered eyelids. She didn't seem impressed.

For the first time, I really noticed Burt's age. I hoped nothing was wrong with him; I had come to depend on him.

I SAT IN THE DIM CORNER of the Viking Hoard hoping no one would see me. I just had to have a moment to think.

What I really needed was a list of who took sleeping pills, or who had sleeping pills in their home prior to Aunt Bee's death. I couldn't believe it when Margaret told me you could buy them at her school from some guy who kept tons of baggies of pills in his locker.

I hated to even think it of such a pretty young thing, but Margaret made a really good suspect. If Bee's will could be overturned, then her family would inherit the whole ten million. Probably the house, the antique car, and the Vardo, too. I briefly wondered if they could sue me for the missing six million.

As much as I wanted to find another suspect, nobody else stood out. Oh, Burt sometimes looked far ragey-er then he should, and I suspected he was entering the first stages of dementia. Poor Burt, although he was over 90, so it wouldn't be too surprising to think his mind was going.

Helen was clearly a closeted lesbian, but I just couldn't see her killing Bee, not even in a jealous rage. I suppose Greta made a halfway decent suspect, at least a part of me hoped she did. I was tired of her crankiness, better-than-thou attitude, and all-over general meanness. But despite her constant belittling of Helen, helping only to drive Helen away from her, she seemed terrified of being alone. I just didn't believe she would kill one of her few friends.

Of course, there were other people on the street who never befriended me, so I really didn't know anything about them. I suppose it could have been one of them. In which case, Miko was on his own because I had no idea who it could be. What if it had been someone entirely different, someone we hadn't even thought of?

Despite her protestations of innocence, there was still a good case for it having been Bee's lawyer and his secretary. After all, they tried to steal every cent the poor woman had. Was it such a stretch to think they would've killed her as well?

I waved the waitress away as she started to move toward me. My coffee had turned cold, but it was much too early for a drink. And I needed a clear head to figure anything out. I made slow finger doodles on the table using the droplets that had condensed from my glass of ice water. They say art can clear your mind and bring forgotten things into focus.

It didn't work.

I don't know how long I sat there staring into my cold coffee, at least long enough for it to congeal and become truly yucky. The girls talked about going back to Ottawa right after Bee's memorial, which was something else unfinished. We still had to pick a date.

I knew I should head home to make sure Victor got his walkies and that supper was started on time. I vaguely recalled it being my night to cook. Maybe I'd just pick up Lebanese food on the way home. I didn't feel like doing anything, and figuring out what to cook, then cooking it, sure seemed like doing something.

What wine pairs well with shawarma?

I was just tucking a ten-dollar bill under my coffee mug when Mom sat down opposite me. You could have knocked me over with a feather.

"Mom, what are you doing here?"

My mother glanced around and waved at the waitress pointing at my coffee cup with her other hand. She pulled out a cotton handkerchief and wiped the table.

"Mom, how did you know I was here?" I paused as the waitress sat down her empty cup, then filled hers, and refilled mine despite me shaking my head. She pulled a handful of creamers out of her apron pocket and dropped them on the table before heading off.

"Oh, Burt said you liked this bar." Mom waved her hand as if brushing away the comment. She glanced around again, clearly taking in the Viking theme, and nodded her approval. One corner of her mouth tilted up as she spied the pretty blond man behind the bar, the same one who'd waited on me the last time I was here.

"I've only been here once before, but I guess it was with Burt." I shrugged. "I must have told him I liked it, but that doesn't explain why you're here."

Mom made a big show out of getting her coffee just the way she liked it before looking up and meeting my eyes. If I didn't know better, I'd say she was uncomfortable and feeling out of place. Although I'd had limited success with the technique before, I decided to outwait her again. This time it worked.

She pushed aside the handkerchief she been fiddling with, took a big swallow of coffee, and met my eyes.

"There are a few things you don't know about Bee. She wasn't always—she was like you."

I reached over and stilled her restless fingers with my own. "I know, Mom. She left me a note along with the house keys. I always suspected anyway. I think that was why she left me everything—because I was like her."

Mom shook her head. "She was like you in more ways than just that. She was very private, especially about her past and there were things she didn't want even you to know." She took another sip of coffee and put the cup down on the saucer with a clunk. "You always had her on such a pedestal, and I guess she liked it there too much to tell you certain things."

I felt my mouth drop open and closed it before Mom could reach over to tap my chin. I had had Bee on a pedestal before, but now I was learning things that made the pedestal crack and shake a bit. "I know she was married and had kids before she came back and became Beatrice. I know she faked her death."

Mom reached over and gripped my hand where it was wrapped around my cold coffee. "I should have known you would know more than I thought." She smiled at me. "You always were the smart one. Oh, don't tell Karey I said that, but you were the one that inherited my brains."

I nodded and smiled back. "I knew that."

Mom chuckled softly. "Do you know why she did? I mean why she faked her death back then?"

I took a sip of coffee and made a face, it might have been warmer, but it was no better tasting. "I figured it was because she needed to start new as Beatrice. She had to make "Brian" disappear in a way that no one would look for him and come up with her." I shrugged again; things were different in the fifties.

"Yes, and no. Bee's wife Mary-Elizabeth was a real—well it sounds like *stitch*. Nothing Bee did was ever enough: didn't pay Mary-Elizabeth enough attention, didn't do enough housework, and certainly didn't make enough money. None of us could understand why Bee married her." She watched her fingers ripping the paper napkin. "Or why she allowed Mary-Elizabeth to push her around. Bee had had a good job here in Smiths Falls, but the *stitch* made Bee move to a job she hated just because it made more money."

This was all news to me. Bee had always been so cheerful, so genuinely happy with life, I had a hard time picturing her henpecked and miserable. Of course, I had some understanding. I had been miserable when everyone thought I was a man, too, but to have an unhappy marriage on top of that must've been horrid.

As if Mom could read my thoughts, she nodded and continued talking. "Of course, I had been shocked when she first came home as Beatrice, but I soon realized she was so much happier, and since no one else recognized her, we just let the neighbors think what they thought. I suppose they assumed she was a cousin."

"Well, aside from the *stitch* for a wife, I already knew that. So, what say we head out and do a little therapeutic shopping? I could use more cookies."

"I haven't told you the most important secret yet."

I shook my head. "That she walked out on her children? I don't understand that, but I know she did. I met them the other day, at least her grandson and his daughter."

Mom glanced around for the waitress but shook her head when the waitress caught her eye. "That wasn't it. That was part of it, but that wasn't why." She deliberately put down the shredded napkin and flexed her hands against the table.

I wondered what could possibly be so difficult for her to say, what could be worse than abandoning your children?

"Victoria, Bee believed that her wife had tried to kill her. She knew the woman had been having an affair with a local man. I mean, local to them, not here."

"What? What do you mean she tried to kill Bee?" I grabbed my Mom by her hand and shook it a little bit. "Didn't Aunt Bee empty the bank accounts, go fishing, then fake her own death?"

"Almost. It was Mary-Elizabeth who emptied the bank accounts and when Bee saw that her wife had taken everything, Bee figured she herself had better disappear. She wasn't certain Mary-Elizabeth would kill her until Bee got their boat out on the lake, and it started leaking. It was a brand-new boat and Bee had made sure it was in good repair the last time she'd used it. Bee said it didn't start leaking until she reached the deepest part of the lake, and then it filled up fast."

After that we sat in silence, thinking everything over. I knew that Mary-Elizabeth had died a number of years ago. Mark had said his father had died last year, so the stalker could be neither of them, since they hadn't been continuously alive for the past 60 years. And there had been no sign Mary-Elizabeth had known that "her husband" had survived. In fact, she had had Bee declared dead almost immediately. So, who had been leaving the threatening notes? No one had actually said it was for the whole sixty years, how long did she actually get them?

I asked Mom. It seemed like something she'd know.

I was not disappointed; Bee had been receiving the notes for just over fifteen years. And since she'd received one the week before her death, it couldn't have been her son or daughter. It could have been Mark, though. He was old enough to have found her and might not have heard about her death right away. Or it could have been Burt. I was only assuming that his dementia was new, as I hadn't known him before inheriting the house.

I looked up at Mom as sadness, anger, and more complex emotions drifted over her face.

"Mom? I can't believe Bee abandoned her kids. She loved Karey and me, so I know she loved them, too."

"She did, with all her heart. But she didn't want to risk her wife finding out she was still alive and coming after her."

I shook my head. She could have sworn them to secrecy.

"Victoria, when was the last time you saw your kids? Five years? Ten?"

I flushed with irritation. *That isn't the same thing. Not at all. For one thing, my kids are in their thirties, not just babies.*

My mother had become an expert at interpreting my expressions during those long teenage years when I rarely spoke to her.

"Victoria, it may not be exactly the same circumstances, but it's close enough for you to show a little empathy. Especially since things were so much more difficult back then."

With that, she gathered her things, leaned over to kiss my forehead and left.

I sighed. I felt guilty about my own kids now. And guilty for judging Bee so harshly. I waved at the waitress for a martini. I had thinking to do.

IT SEEMED TO BE TAKING the waitress a ridiculously long time to come back with my martini. As I looked around the room for her one more time, I saw MacGuinty slouch into the bar and look around.

He gazed at the patrons with that "dead-eyed cop-stare," and I could tell the second his eyes lit up on me, here in my dark corner.

I slid closer to the wall, trying to hide in the darker shadow there. It did not work. After staring at me for a long moment, MacGuinty headed my way.

I deliberately ignored him as I pulled my purse onto the table and pretended to be looking for something. Hopefully, he would get the hint and leave. Unfortunately, it didn't work. MacGuinty reached for something I had placed on the table from my purse, and I slapped at his hand. I froze. Holy spumoni, had I really just slapped MacGuinty?

I slowly raised my gaze to his face. He was not happy. In fact, he looked decidedly unhappy.

"You know that's assault on a police officer, don't you Miss Vee?"

The waitress interrupted before I could think of anything to say, especially since I had no intention of apologizing. In my humble opinion, that man could use a good spanking, unless he would enjoy that. And I was so not going there.

The waitress slid my chilled martinis across the table toward me, and I grabbed it and took a sip. I asked her to make me a double the next time she was on this side of the room. She raised one eyebrow but didn't say anything as she turned to MacGuinty.

"Would you like something, sir? The lunch specials are over in about ten minutes, so you just have time to order something."

"Black coffee."

I was somewhat relieved to see I was not the only one he was so rude to.

He thumped onto the bench opposite me, rested his elbows on the table, and leaned forward, glowering at me.

"A little early to be drinking, ain't it? Trying to drown your guilt?"

I could tell he was trying to be threatening, and he was a little bit, but I also knew he was fishing and had no evidence of me doing anything wrong. Because I hadn't, not one tiny little thing.

"More like drowning my sorrows." I didn't want to say a word to him but somehow I couldn't stop. "After that horrifying debacle at Bee's dis-internment, I haven't been sleeping well."

The waitress arrived with his coffee, and I swear to God, he put in about six sugars. No wonder he had to keep hitching up his belt.

"That much sugar is not good for your health," I said.

"At least it's not sleeping pills." He stared at me to see my reaction.

I paused, stunned that he would just say that. Then my temper rose. I leaned forward, my nose nearly touching his as we were both leaning over the table, glowering at each other.

"You're wasting your time looking at me. I adored Bee. If you want to catch her killer, look into who was her stalker, who was sending her threatening letters, and who had access to sleeping pills."

He leaned back in his seat a smug look on his face, like it gotten me to spill something. He took a loud slurp of his coffee. In my current mood, I found that noise utterly disgusting.

"I checked your records. You had a prescription for sleeping pills."

Well, how the peppermint fudge did he know that? But all I said was, "That prescription was over five years ago, and it was never refilled."

I stuffed everything back into my purse, slid the ten-dollar bill under my coffee cup, and stood up. I towered over him, at least while he was sitting, and made a loud, yet still delicate and ladylike, sniff.

"I'm not doing your job for you again this time. You'll have to work this out for yourself, and PS... it's not me."

With that, I tilted my nose in the air and stalked out. I thought I heard him say, "We'll just see about that," but I ignored him. Punching him wasn't worth the jail time. Although part of me thought it might be worth it.

Chapter Eight

Luci had headed back to Ottawa right after lunch. She'd said she and Jaqi had things to talk about. That did not sound good.

But I had plenty to keep me busy, and she had promised to be back in time for the reburial. I hoped Jaqi would come back with her—I could use all the friends I could get.

When I arrived home, I stayed in the car for a moment. I didn't know why my heart pounded; everything looked normal. But just as I reached for the door handle to get out of the car, I noticed a shadow by the side of the house that didn't look right. It had moved, when none of the other shadows had.

Instead, I rolled down the window and leaned my head out. "Who's there? Come on out, I've already seen you."

I saw the shadow move again and heard someone beat feet out the back. There was a door from my back garden to the street behind. They would be long gone by the time I got there.

I got out of the car and looked around but didn't see anything amiss. So, I decided to forget it.

I checked my front door, and it was still locked, so I opened it and went in. I decided my imagination had been playing tricks on me. Lord knows my nerves were shot.

Speaking of shots, I poured myself a small one of my fanciest gin and relaxed into my armchair. I just needed to shut my brain off for a few hours.

I must have dozed off because the next thing I knew Luci was shaking me awake. She had two suitcases by the door and was biting her lower lip. Her eyes were puffy and red.

"Sweetheart," I said, "what's going on?"

She didn't answer, just crouched at my feet and put her head on my knees. That worried me.

"Luci, did something happen with Jaqi?" Tears filled her eyes and one slipped down the side of her face. "Luci, sweetheart, just tell me what's wrong."

"Oh, Vee. Jaqi just let me leave. We had a fight, and she just let me leave." She sobbed in earnest.

It took a while, but I finally got her calmed down. At least enough to tell me what had happened.

It seemed Jaqi had been putting all of her time and energy into her new book and a new assistant. Luci felt abandoned and had tried to talk to Jaqi about it, but it turned into a fight.

I rested my head on top of hers and wrapped my arms around her. I didn't for a moment believe that Jaqi had stopped loving her, but I understood her fear and pain. This couple had always been so close, like the world contained only the two of them.

I sighed deeply. Things seem to be falling apart all over. First Bee's death and her lawyer being murdered, then the threats against me, and now this.

Chocolate. That was what we needed. I eased Luci off of my lap, then pulled her to her feet. I had to practically drag her, but soon she sat at the kitchen table, and I was busy at the stove mixing cream, cocoa, and real chocolate over the heat.

It only took a few minutes before we sat side-by-side and sipped the rich, creamy drink. Hot chocolate always makes everything better. When Luci seemed calmer, I decided to find out what was really going on.

"She said if I do not trust her, maybe we should take a break. Oh Vee, she is dumping me." Her voice thickened with tears again.

"I'm sure she didn't mean it. People say things when they're angry. I'm as certain as certain can be that she'll call you tomorrow and apologize."

Luci just shook her head and stared miserably into her hot chocolate. I didn't know what else to say. I couldn't believe they were breaking up. Besides being my best friends, they were perfect together. Surely, Jaqi wasn't really cheating on Luci.

I couldn't imagine it.

Had they just drifted apart without my noticing? Jaqi's books had become more successful, and that meant a bigger pull on her time. I understood how Luci could feel abandoned.

LUCI AND I GOT INTO the car and drove to the funeral home. It might be just a reburial, but I still had to pick a new casket and make arrangements.

I hoped it wouldn't take too long because I looked forward to Ben's lunch special at the Bun Journee, which was only available until 2:00 p.m.

Why do all morticians have their hair slicked back, they all look like Gomez Addams. Even the women.

The air smelled too sweet, like lilacs were taking over the world. Bee had loved lilacs, and the strong scent made it seem like she was here with us. I resolved to behave.

The mortician led us down the hall away from the showrooms to his office. He seemed to bow a little bit as he held the door open for Luci and me to enter. He smiled unctuously as he took his place behind his desk.

"How may I help you today, Miss Lilley? I don't really need to be there at the reburial."

I glanced at Luci. This could be awkward since he apparently did not already know about the casket being destroyed. But before I could say anything, he continued talking.

"Are you looking to make arrangements for your own funeral? Pre-planning can take so much weight and pain away from your family at a difficult time. If you pay for everything now, they will even be protected against the prices going up in the future."

"What? Heavens no. I'm still here about Aunt Bee. The police, well, they wrecked her casket. I need a new one before she can be buried again."

I swear I saw money signs in his eyes as he began to smile. I needed to put the kibosh on that right away. Since there was not going to be another funeral, the coffin didn't matter.

"Now, I just need something plain, so that she doesn't get buried in a cardboard box."

A corner of Luci's mouth quirked up, but the mortician looked horrified. I guess she thought I was joking, but Aunt Bee really was being delivered back to the funeral home in a cardboard box.

Once the mortician felt convinced I would not put out thousands of dollars for a fancy new casket, things went rather quickly. We ordered a nice pine coffin, vaguely reminiscent of the old West, and paid for it in less than half an hour.

When Bee was delivered this afternoon, everything would be ready for her. I did, however let him talk me into new flowers. I suppose they went well with the minister saying another service.

At least we still had time to get to the Bun Journee for lunch.

WEDNESDAY MORNING WAS quiet, too quiet. I peeked into the spare bedroom to find Luci still asleep. Victor whined. It was past time for him to go out to widdle.

While Victor played in the fenced backyard, I set about putting on a large pot of coffee and pulled some eggs from the fridge. After a moment's thought, I also grabbed the bacon. Today would need a serious breakfast.

I was just putting the bread in the toaster when Luci shuffled into the kitchen. She looked more rested but not happier than she had yesterday.

"Morning Luci, breakfast will be ready in just a second. We should be ready to go in about 40 minutes, as Burt will be here to pick us up right at nine."

She looked like she was about to say something but changed her mind, grabbing a mug from the cupboard. Once her coffee was to her liking, Luci sat down at the table again. Moments later, I placed a plateful of bacon, eggs, frozen hash-browns and toast in front of her. I sat beside her, and we both tucked in, eating quickly as she still needed to get dressed.

To be fair, I wasn't ready either.

ALL TOO SOON, A KNOCK at the door brought me scurrying downstairs. Burt was here already, at barely past quarter-to. I yelled up the stairs for Luci to hurry and opened the door.

"Come in, I just need to put on my shoes and find my jacket."

He nodded and stepped in, closing the door behind him.

I realized I had left Victor in the backyard. With my shoes in my hand, I hurried to the back door and opened it, prepared to call or go searching for my poor puppy.

The second the door was open, Victor came barreling in, covered in mud from tip of his nose to tip of his tail. There was a bright pink rose petal on top of his head.

"Oh Victor, what have you done?" I looked toward the roses that lined the side of the yard and could see not one bloom. The last time I looked, they had been covered in flowers. I looked down at Victor and frowned at his happily wagging tail.

"What did you do?" I repeated, then I heard Luci running down the stairs and realized there was no time to worry about the back yard. "You and I will talk about this later, young man."

In deference to his muddy, well, everything, I shut him in the downstairs bathroom. I would think about this later.

Chapter Nine

We were all back at the graveyard with the heavy machinery and Miko on one side of the grave, the rest of us standing about ten yards away on the other.

The déjà vu felt strong today, as it seemed to be all the same people doing all the same things. Only this time, the machinery would do everything in reverse.

I sat on my walker, missing Victor's comforting presence. My poor roses—what a bad dog he had been. What had gotten into him? He had never been interested in my flowers before.

Footsteps on gravel caught my attention, and I glanced up to see Greta and Helen arriving with the priest and his assistant, again.

I must've looked disapproving because Greta caught my eye and scowled. She strongly resembled Squinty MacGuinty, Miko's old police partner who disapproved of everything and only had one expression—scowling.

At least it wasn't raining today. I crossed my fingers hoping not to jinx it as I looked up at a bright sun and hazy clouds.

Ben handed me a takeout cup of coffee and an almond croissant. He had pulled his van as close to us as he could and seemed to have half of his café packed into the back. There were half a dozen bright pink boxes, which obviously held pastries, and two commercial-sized urns of coffee.

When he told people to help themselves, you would think that a riot broke out as everyone juggled for position to be the first to get an éclair or chocolate croissant.

Ben looked a little horrified, but then he was such a sweet, gentle boy. Unlike Victor, who was in the doghouse this morning.

The front-end-loader-earthmover-whatever started with a loud growl. Everyone's attention switched to watch the machine as it tidied up the grave hole. I could see Aunt Bee's new pine coffin sitting under a green tarp to one side. It was sad to think that her whole life had come down to this, a half a dozen neighbors and a plain, pine box.

When the machine operator paused, Miko glanced at me, and then nodded. The operator swung down from the door of his machine to pull the tarp off of the coffin. He hooked up several chains to the side handles and then to the front of the machine.

I held my breath as the coffin swung up into the air, remembering its disturbing fall to earth last time. This time nothing went wrong however, and the coffin was soon tucked tidily into its hole.

I only realized I still held my breath when my head got a bit muzzy, and my lungs started burning. I released it slowly, not wanting to faint this time.

The workmen switched front-ends on the great machine and started filling in the grave. Miko headed toward our group, and I realized everything was over. I felt grateful that the re-internment had been uneventful, but after this week, it seemed a bit of a letdown.

I turned my back on the priest striding toward the grave, bible in hand. I'd resolved to say nothing to Greta about this because it appeared to be a big thing for her. She was mourning, too.

Helen helped Ben pick up the bits of napkin and empty paper cups and stow them in the back of his van. I wondered what everybody would do now. More importantly, I wondered where the heck Jaqi was. She had promised to be here.

I didn't want to get in the middle of her and Luci's fight, but between Jaqi's absence and Luci's sad eyes, I started to get angry.

SOMEHOW, EVERYONE ENDED up back at my place, again. If this kept up, I would soon run out of coffee. And I would need a bigger teapot. Do they make ten-cup teapots?

I dragged Luci into the kitchen to help me put on a few nibblies. I was out of cookies, but maybe Ben had a few pastries left. This crowd ate more than Victor after a walk.

Luci stopped dead the moment she walked into the kitchen, and I walked straight into her back. For a moment, I hoped this meant Jaqi had been waiting for us, but when I peered over Luci's shoulder, the room was empty.

"Oh no, Vee." Luci pointed at the sliding door onto the patio. It was standing partly open and the wood by the lock had been shattered. There were bits and pieces of wood on the dining room floor. It looked like the door had been yanked hard enough for the lock to pull straight out of the wood. But who would be strong enough to do that?

And why?

MIKO AND I FINISHED checking the house, but nothing seemed to be missing or misplaced. He shrugged, and I frowned at him. He just turned and walked down the stairs toward his husband.

I followed him but paused halfway down. It sounded like a voice had just spoken in my mind: *Aunt Bee had been poisoned.*

What if someone had broken in to poison me? And all those people downstairs eating my food and drinking my coffee.

I grabbed Miko's shoulder to tell him what I was thinking, but it seemed the same thought had occurred to him. He shrugged off my hand and ran for the kitchen.

"Nobody touch anything." Ben was in the middle of pouring three cups of coffee, but he paused to look at Miko. Carefully placing the coffee pot back on the burner, he then looked over Miko's shoulder at me.

"Someone broke in while we were out." My hand shakily pointed at the patio door. Ben turned and nodded.

I could see his thoughts play across his expressive face before he smiled tightly. "The coffee in the van should be still hot, and there are still a few pastries. People should be going home for lunch soon anyway."

Miko smiled grimly. "I could hurry them along if you wish." From the living room I could hear Greta's raised voice criticizing Burt for something. I didn't mind at all.

But I shook my head. I could get them out easier, faster, and with less fuss myself.

I heard Miko speaking on the phone, presumably to report the break-in. I just watched Greta make uncomfortable people even more miserable with her sharp tongue. I wouldn't need to do a thing; people would be fleeing in droves.

And as soon as they did, I would do a more thorough check of the house.

IT WAS LATE AFTERNOON, Constable Smith had come, taken my report, and left. Ben had had to go back to the café, and Miko had gone back to work. There was just myself and Luci left.

While we waited for the contractor to come fix the patio door, we sat and watched a little TV. *Frosted Flakes in orange Jell-O!* Daytime TV. I could feel my brain shrinking.

The house phone rang, startling Victor from his nap on the couch. I hadn't had the heart to really punish him; he probably wouldn't have understood me anyway. My hip protested a little as I leaned sideways to grab the phone off the cradle.

"Hello?" All I heard was dead air and possibly breathing. "Hello?" I used a sterner voice to try to force them to answer me.

It didn't work. I gave it a few more seconds and then hung up.

I had just gotten sucked into a weird courtroom show with an opinionated bald man as the judge, when the phone rang again. Luci met my eyes, and this time, she reached to answer it. It was apparently dead air again because she frowned and hung up.

"I think it is a bored teenager. Although it might be Jaqi. She has a hard time saying sorry."

I nodded, but something told me it was neither. We sent out for pizza for supper since I had thrown everything in the fridge into the garbage. I knew I was probably overdoing it, but since I didn't know whether anything had been drugged, it all had to go.

I had bought a portable doorbell online a few weeks ago—the ringer was portable, the bell stayed attached to the door—and I decided to test it with the pizza guy.

Before we got out the back door, the phone rang again. We both stopped to stare at it like it was some alien device we'd never seen before. It rang a second time, and I shuffled into the kitchen to grab the extension.

"Whoever this is, you are not being as amusing as you think. I have things to do and have no time for your foolishness."

"MacGuinty's voice lazily oozed out of the receiver. "Well now Miss Vee, that's rather ungrateful, considering I didn't file a report on your assault on me at that seedy bar."

"Assault? I never touched you. I merely tried to slap your hand, and you moved too fast for me to hit." I took a deep breath trying to calm myself. It would do no good to make him angry. "Never mind. What can I help you with today, Lieutenant?"

"I was just calling to give you fair warning that if there's anything you want to tell me, you better do it now. I'm just about ready to file charges."

Ready to file charges? He couldn't really be ready, there could be no evidence.

"Well Officer, you do what you have to do. While I wait for you to embarrass yourself again, I have things to accomplish. So, I guess I'll see you when I see you."

I gently laid the receiver down and leaned over to rest my hands on the counter and remind myself to breeze. He'd arrested me on zero evidence before, I wouldn't be surprised if he did it again. Maybe I should call Miko, but he had said he wasn't on the case because of our friendship. I took a deep breath, stood up straight, slipped my hands over my hips to straighten the hem of my pretty pink sequined T-shirt, and told myself that tomorrow would be another day.

I nodded to Luci to let her know I was okay and grabbed a bottle of water to take outside.

I had remembered my roses and carried the buzzer with me to check on them. Luci followed me out with Victor on his leash because she also didn't trust him to stay out of the flowers. But the more I looked at the roses, the less I thought Victor had done it.

There were marks on the branches below where the buds had been that looked like they had been made by hitting the plant with a stick. They were definitely not tooth marks. And the plants had not been dug up, which was Victor's favourite gardening trick.

But why would anyone have taken a stick to my plants, especially my beautiful roses? "Who did you piss off, baby?"

Luci glanced back at me, a small smile hovering over her lips. "I would be very worried if they ever answered you."

I opened my mouth to answer when the buzzer rang. For a second, I thought I had made that noise. Then Luci grinned and yelled, "Pizza," taking off for the front door of the house.

At least some things never changed.

SOON ENOUGH IT WAS bedtime, and since Luci had worn herself out with crying, we decided to forgo hot chocolate and a movie in favor of sleeping.

Of course, we didn't go straight to sleep. We stayed up, putting avocado masks on our faces and curlers in Luci's beautiful long hair. And tried to talk things out.

Apparently, I had been too focused to notice the beginnings of their falling out; it had started on our camping trip last month. Luci's nervousness had made her a bit clingy, and Jaqi's writing frenzy had made her aloof. This had left Luci feeling uncertain about their relationship and Jaqi feeling claustrophobic. I had assumed they had worked everything out after being kidnapped, but I'd been wrong about that.

Over the past three weeks, Jaqi had escaped what she thought was Luci's over protectiveness by spending more time writing in coffee shops and with her new assistant. While Luci had battled her insecurity by cooking fancy meals and arranging romantic evenings together.

Apparently, it never occurred to either one to simply talk to each other.

VICTOR HAPPILY SNORED and farted on his side of my queen-size bed, and I was half-asleep with a cheap romance novel resting on my nose. When the phone rang, I just about hit the ceiling.

Being startled out of my skin had always made me cranky, so I wasn't the politest when I answered the phone.

"Hello, who is this?" I heard the peevishness in my voice and pulled Victor into a hug to try to calm down.

"Hello? Is this Victoria? This is Helen."

"Helen, what time is it? Is everything okay?" Something must be off because she should've been in bed hours ago.

Victor snuffled for a moment, then passed gas and curled up asleep on my side of the bed. Carl had been right; this dog really was a fart machine.

Since I was paying attention to Victor, I missed the first few words Helen said, but I wasn't about to admit it. So, I forced myself to listen, thinking I could pick up what I missed from the context.

"She didn't feel the same, but she was such a lovely woman that I couldn't help it. Of course, I knew Greta was jealous of the time I spent with her. And I know I talked about her too much. But still, don't you think she overreacted?"

I couldn't think of a thing to say—I really needed to know what her first sentence had been. She could be talking about anything.

"I'm sorry, Helen, I missed the first thing you said. Would you mind repeating it?"

There was silence on the line except for a soft sigh. "I'm so sorry, dear, were you asleep?"

That sounded as good an excuse as any, so I agreed that I had been asleep. Someday I would have to learn how to pay attention and not let my mind wander.

"I suppose I just wanted someone to talk to that wasn't Greta. She's been acting so odd and touchy lately." She sighed softly again. "I just miss Bee so much, I guess Greta is sick of hearing about it. But don't you think she overreacted?"

I still didn't know what Greta had done but based on her earlier behavior, I was on Helen's side 100%. I told her so.

"I don't know that I can forgive her for calling Bee weird. Bee was her own person. I thought she was very brave."

I made agreeable noises and assured Helen that she wasn't being foolish, and eventually she felt better enough that we could hang up.

Of course, by now I was awake, and Victor was sleeping in my spot.

I WAS AWAKENED WAY too early by the phone ringing—again. It felt like I had barely gotten the sleep after Helen's call, and here someone else expected me to be polite to them. I gritted my teeth and rolled, reaching for the nightstand, which was much farther away than I expected. For some reason, I'd been sleeping on Victor's side of the bed, and my side of the bed had the sheets all pulled into a curl, although there was no Victor there.

"Hello?" My voice was scratchy enough to be mistaken for Burt next door. There was silence on the line for a moment, so I used that time to clear my throat. I thought I might be catching a cold, as clearing my throat became cough, and started to sound like I had been smoking a pack-a-day.

"Hello, Miss Vee?"

I thought I recognized Miko's voice. There was no water glass on my bedside table, so I scooched to the edge of the bed and stood up. I realized I had never responded. I agreed that it was me as I padded down the hall toward the stairs.

"I didn't wake you, did I?" He didn't give me time to respond as he ploughed ahead with his findings about the break-in. "We got a lot of nice clear fingerprints, including yours. But I'm going to need exclusion prints from everyone who was there."

"How are you going to do that?" I couldn't picture Greta began happy about being fingerprinted at the police station, and I said as much.

"I hoped you could find a way to do that. Maybe put aside something each of them has touched. I'll come lift the prints."

He had the same tone in his voice as a small child trying to wheedle cookies out of his grandmother. But as I wanted to know who had broken in, I pushed down my instinctive no and agreed to try. Although I had no idea how I was going to accomplish this. On TV, people just put aside the wineglass or coffee cup the suspect had been drinking out of. But I was supposed to fingerprint half a dozen people. How would I keep them straight?

Of course, I had been wondering this while Miko was still talking, so I missed his instructions on how to do it.

I decided my morning had been bad enough without admitting that yet again I wasn't listening, so I decided to fake it until I made it. *Isn't that what young people do nowadays?* Either way, it surely couldn't be too difficult to put spoons and coffee cups into baggies. I think I even had a marker somewhere, so I could write their names on the bags.

After Miko hung up, I pulled out the fresh bag of coffee Luci had picked up yesterday and started a pot. That made me wonder where Luci and Victor were. Victor should've been whining at the door, either to get out or come in. I glanced into the backyard but couldn't spot them.

While my coffee pot emitted rude noises, I went to the front of the house to look out into the yard. There was still no sign of them, and now I felt a little worried. Luci had done a brief grocery run late yesterday, so we had everything we needed for breakfast and lunch. Of course, I had thrown out things like sugar and mayonnaise, so she might be doing a bigger grocery run. But would they have let Victor into the store? She wouldn't have left him in her car or tied up to the front door of the store, so where were they?

The coffee pot made a few more disgruntled hisses, then quieted down. So, I went back to the kitchen to pour myself a cup. If they hadn't turned up by the time I finished, I was determined to go out and find him. There was just too much going on for me to be blasé about Luci's disappearance.

Chapter Ten

Of course, I had barely sat down when the front door opened, and Luci and Victor tumbled in with a lot of noise and laughter.

I carried my cup into the living room planning to give them a *how could you have worried me this much for no reason* stare.

Luci looked happy. I swallowed my snarky remark and set my coffee on top of the TV. Victor bounced around her feet at the end of his rainbow-coloured leash. Luci met my eyes and positively lit up.

"Jaqi texted. She's coming to get me." Luci practically hopped over to me and gave me a big hug. Her cheeks were flushed, and her eyes were sparkling like a little kid on Christmas morning. This news also excited Victor, who decided to run around and tangle his leash around both of us, tying us together so neither could reach down to untangle it.

I was so relieved they were working it out. Mama hates it when the kids fight.

Luci was in such a good mood, she went all out making a brunch to rival anything at the Bun Journee. Spicy omelets with fresh tomatoes, sweet peppers, and cheese; fresh rolls that she made from scratch; and, fried slices of ham. I was in gastronomical heaven.

While this made up for her disappearing act this morning, it didn't really answer the question of where she had gone. Or why she had left the house so early in the morning.

Actually, it wasn't that early in the morning. If Miko hadn't phoned, my bladder would've woken me up soon enough. Since it was 11:00 a.m. now, it must've been close to 9:00 a.m. when I got downstairs. I couldn't believe I'd overslept; I never do that. Of course, Helen's 1:00 a.m. phone call might have had something to do with it.

That reminded me, I needed get their fingerprints. My heart rate picked up—this would be just like on one of my TV shows. I would need Luci to help. If only so that she didn't wash the dishes I hid in the kitchen.

We were halfway through making a plan to get people over here one at a time, so we didn't confuse coffee cups, when a quick rap at the door sounded, and Jaqi bounced in.

Luci squealed and jumped up to run over and hug Jaqi. Jaqi wrapped her arms around Luci and kissed her soundly on the mouth. I felt my eyes tear up, feeling intense relief. All was right in my world again.

Except for, you know, Bee having been murdered and someone threatening me and the house being broken into. I shook these thoughts away with a toss of my spiky head. This was a good day; the girls were back together.

THAT AFTERNOON, THE three of us made a huge grocery run. It reminded me of the groceries I had bought soon after moving into the house, that is, we bought way too much. Even though I had thrown out almost everything in the kitchen, there just wasn't room for all of the cookies, frozen treats, and fun new tea blends. I had so much fun buying groceries. Putting them away, not so much.

Then, I had a brilliant idea.

To celebrate Jaqi's arrival, we could have a tea party. It was a good thing I thought of this while we were still out, since I decided to get a different coloured teacup for each person, to make it easier to remember which fingerprints belonged to whom. All we had to do was convince everyone to come over, and hope they weren't so sick of each other that they refused.

Apparently, I had overlooked the lure of free food. Everyone agreed to be there after supper for dessert and tea. They'd have come for dinner if they could've gotten away with it. I had to be very clear with my invitation, especially with Burt. Luci and Jaqi had disappeared upstairs after we got all the groceries put away, no doubt to have their own celebration.

I distracted myself with first deciding who gets what colour of teacup, and then making fresh peanut butter cookies. I just hoped I could resist eating them all before people started arriving. Peanut butter cookies were my weakness, well, all cookies were my weakness. Especially with a nice cup of tea.

I probably should have staggered people's arrival, as once more my living room was so crowded, no one could move. At least I hadn't had to bring in all of my dining room chairs this time. Who knew my collection of antique teapots could be so useful? I put a different blend in each one; the Brown Betty had a nice, sturdy English Breakfast, the pink and silver lace teapot that matched my dishes had one of my favourite blends, and the cute one shaped like a dragon, obviously, had Dragon Gunpowder tea.

That last one had enough caffeine to have my heart pounding and my eyes bugged out. At least I no longer felt tired. I might have been talking a little too fast, though, because Burt kept asking me to repeat myself, and Luci kept laughing at me.

My color-coded cups and saucers had turned out to be a brilliant idea. Helen and Burt thought it was so cute to have matching dessert plates, and even Greta thought it handy. Especially after she went to the bathroom and found her plate and cup in a different location than she had left them. It was her own fault; they were taking up prime real estate on the coffee table and both were empty. How was I to know she had planned on second helpings?

So, of course, she found her dishes in a large freezer bag, and I had to admit everything. She was not pleased, no, not pleased at all.

She grabbed the bag of dishes from my hand and tore the bag, ripping it open. She yanked open the cupboard door under the sink and grabbed my rubber gloves and a bottle of dish soap. Running a bit of hot water, she scrubbed the dishes thoroughly.

After practically scrubbing the color from the edges of the plate and teacup, she tossed the dishcloth into the sink and turned to glare at me.

"There, see what you can lift from *that*." And she stomped from the sink straight down the hall to the front door and out.

Burt stared at me for a moment then shrugged. He had been standing there holding his dishes, but now he picked up the dishcloth and washed them. He looked apologetic as he carefully set them in the drainer and dried his hands.

"Sorry about this Vee, but I can't be having my fingerprints splashed all over the place. Even old men have a history."

"The only history I care about is who broke in the other day, who trashed my roses, and who murdered Aunt Bee." I gave him my best Queen Elizabeth stare, the one that freezes terrorists in their shoes and makes even little princes behave. "I would've thought you would want to know that, too. Seeing as how you're always talking about being sweet on her—unless you *had been* involved in her death." I lowered my brows and gave him the evil eye.

Burt pursed his lips, shuffled his feet, looked me in the eye, then sighed explosively. "Dang it, Vee. You know that woman was the light of my life. I would never have hurt her." He shoved his hands deep into his pockets and appeared to be talking to his feet. "I can't make no promises for what my fingerprints turn up, but I'd never hurt my girl. Course, you got no reason to believe that do you?"

In a move that surprised me, Burt picked up the plate from the dish rack leaving a perfect set of prints. He even licked the edge and grinned at me.

"Just in case they need some of that DNR evidence."

I smiled and reached over to give him a little hug, when over his head I saw Helen staring at me with big eyes. *Trotting tiger tails!* Now I would have to explain to *her* what I was doing.

"You don't suspect us, do you?" Helen's voice wavered a little bit, and I wasn't sure if it was from tears or fear. Considering how Greta had stomped out, I shouldn't have been surprised.

"Of course not. Miko needed exclusionary prints, and I guess I got all wrapped up in playing secret agent. I'm sorry, I should have just asked."

WELL, LEAVE IT TO BURT, he soon had everyone lining up to give me their fingerprints, making sure I spelled their name right on the little baggie. I felt bad for not inviting him into our secret spy clique earlier. Of course, it wasn't that secret anymore.

I called Miko to tell him to come pick up the fingerprints and let him know that Greta had been fit to be tied and refused. I let him think everyone else had volunteered rather than being tricked. It was sort of true, and far less embarrassing than having been caught out.

He told me he would drop by on his way to work the next day and asked me to figure out how to get Greta's prints as well. Unless there was some reason she didn't want him to have them.

Based on her reaction, I had to assume there was a reason, but I was *French vanilla'd* if I could figure out what it was. Other than the obvious.

The fingerprinting—and having to tell everyone why—soon put the kibosh on the rest of the party. *I guess it's difficult to drink tea and eat cookies while your hostess thinks you're a murderer.*

I felt just as pleased, though. The day had taken its emotional toll, and I suddenly felt exhausted. The caffeine had left me jittery, but my brain had turned into cooked cauliflower. I just hoped I could sleep.

At least I didn't have any dishes to wash.

VICTOR WOKE ME UP THE next morning, barking and scratching at my closed bedroom door. I shuffled over to open the door, thinking he needed to take a wee, but instead of heading for the kitchen, he barked his way to the front door.

Despite the cheerful birds outside the windows, it was still very early. So, I might not have been my most gracious when I opened the door and saw Helen nibbling at a fingernail and looking guilty.

She had been gazing toward the street, and my opening the door must've startled her because she spun back to me and nearly toppled off the step.

"Hey, easy there." I reached out to grab her elbow before she went flying. It was only as I caught her arm that I realized her hands were full of dishes.

"Greta just finished breakfast. Here." She pushed the dishes toward me, and I reached out instinctively to take them. Once they were in my hands, I realized they would now be covered in fingerprints. Hers, mine, and Greta's. Hopefully, Helen hadn't stopped at anyone else's house on the way here.

She still fidgeted with the neck of her dress and muttered about needing to get back before Greta became suspicious, when a long black car pulled into my driveway.

It was Miko's unmarked police car. Though, everyone knew that the only Crown Vic's in Smiths Falls were police cars.

Helen nodded and smiled at Miko uncertainly as she passed him on her way back to the sidewalk. He smiled back, his eyes tracking her until she passed the hedge.

"What brings her here so early in the morning?" he asked, then hopped up the three stairs to kiss me on the cheek and slide past me into the house.

"Same thing as you—fingerprints. Would you like a cup of coffee?"

I waited for a moment for Victor to finish his business in the front yard, then closed the door and padded my disheveled self into the kitchen to start coffee.

I didn't wait to hear if Miko wanted coffee or not—I needed it. So of course, all of my teacups were in bags waiting to go to the station. No matter, today called for a huge earthenware mug.

Chapter Eleven

The girls had come home with flushed cheeks and giggles. For some reason, it made me wonder what we were doing for Christmas this year, as we had always celebrated it together. But since we hadn't even made it to Halloween yet, I decided not to ask.

Luci had something going in the kitchen that smelled wonderful, and Jaqi and I sat in the parlor, sipping on beautifully chilled martinis. I couldn't wait to tell them about Mark and Margaret, although I didn't want to have to say everything twice, so I waited until Luci joined us. I could see an open bottle of red wine on the half wall, and I knew Luci would drink that.

I could feel the knots and muscles in my shoulders relax and sighed deeply. My cell rang, jolting me out of my bliss. Why had I chosen that annoying song for my ringtone?

Leaning over, I grabbed the phone off the coffee table and poked a little green icon. "Hello, this is me."

Jaqi giggled. I glanced over at her and stuck my tongue out. There was a small chance we should have waited until after we ate before drinking the martinis.

"Hello, Vee? This is Miko. I have the fingerprint results."

That brought my mood down fast. I gestured at the phone for him to keep going before remembering he couldn't see me.

"What did you find? Did the stalker break in? Am I in danger?"

Jaqi leaned forward, a look of concern on her pretty face.

"No," said Miko. "There were no unknown fingerprints. Are you certain someone broke in at all?" He sounded the way I did when speaking to a 100-year-old woman, that is, if I had suspected her brain might not be braining that day.

"No, Miko, it was all a joke. I broke my own door lock and slaughtered Victor's look-alike up in my bedroom. I guess I'll do anything to have a cute guy up there." Okay, that might have been a little snarky, and maybe he didn't deserve it, but how dare he ask if I was sure someone had broken in? He had seen the broken door lock himself.

"Okay, okay, I had to ask. You know this means it was one of your friends, right?"

Well, fudge sticks. He was right. "Are you sure your men checked everywhere for fingerprints?"

Now *he* sounded touchy when he confirmed they had checked everywhere, especially places like the door handle. I didn't want to argue with him, so I made all the appropriate apologetic-sounding noises. Then something occurred to me.

"Did they test my bedroom doorknob? Whoever broke in was in my room."

Luci had come into the room, staring at me with round eyes. I didn't want to worry her, so I shook my head and mouthed Miko at her. It didn't seem to help as her brows drew together and she leaned down to whisper at Jaqi. I waggled my brows at them, meaning I didn't want to be left out of any conversations. Jaqi waggled hers back at me, meaning Lord only knows what.

Since Miko had no idea whether they had fingerprinted my bedroom, he told us to stay downstairs and that he would send someone in a minute. Or in the next two hours at the very least. I agreed, since that gave us time for supper and time to make another pitcher.

I DROVE OVER TO THE neighborhood grocery store, as I was once again out of cookies and cream for coffee. Of course, that's not all I bought. I picked up a little milk for Jaqi since she preferred it to cream in her tea, and I picked up a lovely, whole chicken they had on sale for tonight's supper.

As I walked out, I noticed a group of girls in brown uniforms selling bundles of flowers. For some reason, it reminded me of the little match girl, probably because it was so cold, and they had so few people stopping to buy.

My walker seat was covered in bags of groceries, but I still went over and looked at their selection of flowers. I found a bunch of mums in shades of purple and blue with bits of greenery. It was so pretty, I told them I had to have it.

So, they made a twenty-dollar arrangement, and I was excited for how pretty the table was going to be tonight. It worked out for everybody.

At least until I looked up and saw MacGuinty leaning against my car. What the *pistachio butter-cream* was he doing here? My good mood fled and by the time I'd pushed my walker over the potholes and uneven pavement, my mood had definitely made a downturn.

"Yeah, I thought I saw you in there." MacGuinty had his arms crossed and his chin stuck out. Somehow this made his simple words sound like a threat and an accusation at the same time.

"Okay, you caught me. I was buying groceries. Am I under arrest now? Has buying flowers become a crime?" I knew I was being foolish and that poking the bear was a really bad idea in light of his threats the other day. But this narrow-minded, single track, train wreck of a police officer was really harshing my mellow. Not that things had been very mellow to begin with. He probably didn't even have to work at it, and that just annoyed me even more.

He grinned as if he had really caught me doing something wrong.

"What?" I asked. The longer I stood there, the more he grinned. I recognize the move from all of the mystery shows I'd seen, but dang-it, it worked. It took an effort to smile as if I wasn't concerned at all about his presence. Suddenly, I desperately wanted to chew my nails, but have you seen how much a good manicure costs?

"Oh, I just wanted to make sure you knew I was watching you. What was that old song, everywhere you go, everything you do, I'll be watching you?"

"That was The Police. And I'm glad you will be watching me. It should bore you off your rocker and prove that I'm not doing anything illegal. I still can't believe you're wasting so much time on me while the real killer has time to walk to California."

MacGuinty spat on the pavement near my car. How gross was that?

"Oh, you've already disposed of the body, so I don't expect you to do anything too obvious. But you'll give yourself away somehow; you're just not that smart." And with that, MacGuinty stuck a toothpick in his mouth, wiggled it up and down with his teeth, and strode off toward his police car. I was glad to see the back of him, though I worried about what ridiculous notions he would come up with about my taking garbage out or digging up this season's plants in the garden.

I fought the temptation to start doing perfectly normal things in a suspicious manner. Like carrying out four or five green garbage bags each with something small but heavy to make it look like a cut-up body. It really was not a good idea. *I'm not sure I'm gonna listen to me.*

Chapter Twelve

So, the only fingerprints on my bedroom doorknob were mine and Luci's, which probably meant that the intruder had worn gloves. Which in turn, meant that all those fingerprints had been taken for nothing. Just fabulous.

All this completely changed my mood, and I no longer felt like giggling. It had been one heck of a long day, filled with way more questions than answers and was both frustrating and exhausting. If I hadn't already been home, I would've wanted to go home. Jaqi and Luci had stopped their whispering and giggling and just watched me. I'd had enough to drink to have no idea what to say to them. My brain seemed to have both slowed way down and sped way up.

And something else was bugging me, but I had forgotten completely what it was.

The girls were back to normal by the times we finished tidying up from supper and shared the last bottle of wine. I had about an inch of martini left in my glass and was about to get up to make more when someone knocked at the front door.

Victor raced from under my chair where he had been hoping for fallen crumbs and barked and yipped his way to the entranceway. I yelled at him to hush; his yipping went straight through my head. He did have the grace to look embarrassed and immediately tried to woof instead.

I was surprised to see my mom and Aunt Kay dressed for company on the other side of the door. I didn't remember inviting them. *Oh, cheese balls.* That was what I had forgotten: everyone was coming over at seven for the final, formal meeting about Bee's memorial. Well... *fudge.*

By 6:55 p.m., all the usual suspects had arrived. Ben had carried chairs in from the dining room and remarked that pretty soon, they would be sleeping over—they'd been here that often. I laughed and swatted him in the arm, although the thought did give me a quiver of fear. I treasured my alone time and hadn't had any in what felt like weeks. Not that I minded the girls being here; in fact, I was quite enjoying myself. It was the constantly being surrounded by neighbors, who were lovely people on their own, but a bit much all together in my tiny parlor.

Luci had hurriedly made a couple of pots of tea and dug out the cookies we had just bought. Including my favourite maple creams. Oh well, there were more at the store. Once everyone had their tea and their nibblies, they settled down quickly. I had to admit, I'd be glad when all this was over, if nothing else, it was costing me a fortune in baked goods.

My mother immediately took center stage and read out minutes that nobody had noticed her taking. I hadn't even known we had minutes of the last meeting because it had dissolved in such confusion. On the other hand, it was nice to know that someone had been paying attention to the recent get-together. My mother called for a show of hands to accept the minutes, and I realized we were a lot more organized than I had thought. We had agreed to split the cost of the new funeral arrangement of roses and lilies, and Burt would bring a boombox, of all things, to play music on once we decided what we were playing.

Luci elbowed me in the ribs and gestured for me to raise my hand. I'd lost track of what was being discussed, but since most other people had their hands up, I just simply agreed and raised mine. I was about to get more tea when there was a loud businesslike knock at the door.

I waved my mother to keep going and altered course for the front of the house. Peeking cautiously through the curtained window beside the door, I recognize Mark and Margaret. What on earth were they doing here? Well, there was no help for it; I had to open the door to find out.

In the thirty or so minutes since I last opened the door, the temperature had dropped precipitously. So had the sun, and it was nearly full dark now. I couldn't keep them standing in the chilly breeze, so I invited them in.

As soon as the door shut behind them, they both started taking off their coats and scarves.

"We're just getting together to discuss arrangement for Aunt Bee's memorial." If I had hoped they would apologize for interrupting and leave, I sorely mistaken. Mark ran a hand through his hair, and it fell into a perfectly tousled mop. In the split second I was distracted by wishing my hair would do that, Margaret had walked boldly into the living room and taken my seat.

Mark awkwardly patted my shoulder, and I had no choice but to lead him into the parlor.

"Mom, Aunt Kay, everyone, this is Mark and his daughter Margaret." I pointed at Margaret as I said her name and she smiled politely. I have to admit that felt slightly unnerving.

Mark gave an indecisive wave and nodded at my mom and aunt. "So lovely to meet you all, I'm very sorry we're late, but I had a little car trouble. Seems a piece fell off of my car engine—no idea how that happened." He chuckled awkwardly and glanced around for a place to sit. Not seeing one, he gestured at Margaret to give him her seat, and she scowled but complied. Luci immediately jumped up to give me her seat and sat on the floor at Jaqi's feet.

I glanced at Ben. *Had I invited them here?* He smiled back at me, so I guess I had. I caught Mom staring at Mark with a very puzzled expression that turned to a complete frown as she looked back at me. I didn't feel like explaining anything just then, so I leaned forward and rapped my knuckles on the coffee table.

"So, Mark. I'm sure I mentioned that we reburied my Aunt Bee this week. We're just deciding what to do to make a little ceremony for her. It would be so sad to just bury her and pretend nothing had happened."

Mark nodded. Margaret, perched on the arm of his chair, also nodded and tried to seem like she wasn't bored. She almost succeeded.

"We've already selected a single large bouquet to put on her grave," I said. "I believe we were just discussing the music."

My mother nodded, pleased I'd been paying attention.

Greta demanded to know who the newcomers were and grumped a bit when I introduced them as cousins. Aunt Kay still looked puzzled, but my mother paled when she realized whose children they must be. She narrowed her eyes at me, and I nodded, smiling hesitantly. I really should have talked to her about this, but I had totally forgotten they were coming. If I had even invited them.

But if I hadn't, who had? I shook my head, mentally smacking myself in the forehead. It seemed Burt wasn't the only one having memory troubles.

Mom gave me an expression, which I knew meant we would discuss this later, and went back to chairing the meeting. I didn't recall asking her to take charge either, but I was glad she did. She had the music, the refreshments, and who was doing what worked out and agreed to in no time. Soon everyone was headed for the door, and it was time for me to face the music, so to speak. It might yet end up a funeral dirge.

While the girls and my aunt Kay tidied up, Mark pulled me aside. "I'm sorry if my being here was awkward, I guess I was hoping to get some more answers." He pulled his hand through his hair again and again it fell perfectly into place. "I guess if I wanted answers, I should have asked some questions, eh?"

I watched my mother pushing the chairs back into the dining room for a moment and then smiled. "Why don't you stay and ask them?" Oh, I knew I was going to pay for this. Mom would be livid I hadn't warned her but then she hadn't been answering her phone, had she?

"THAT'S IT! I'M MAKING more martinis." I shook off Luci's restraining hand and strode to the kitchen. Tea was nowhere near strong enough to deal with this conversation. Between Aunt Kay's tears and my mom's refusal to meet Mark's eyes, I was ready to throw the lot of them right out the front door.

Jaqi followed me to the kitchen and quietly started rinsing plates to put in the dishwasher. I glanced at her as I pulled out the fixings for my martinis and realized how rigid her back was. Was she angry at me, too?

"I should've told you about Mark and Margaret before they showed up shouldn't I?"

"Yes," said Jaqi. "You should have." She dumped a handful of silverware into the basket, hard enough to have them ringing like bells. "But you really should have told your mother. How could you not even mention it?"

"I kind of forgot that I hadn't told you, I mean, you and Luci were so busy patching things up and were hardly ever here, I guess it just slipped my mind."

"That's hardly an excuse for not telling your mom. How do you think she feels? Finding out now that Bee had children?" She stuffed the coffee cup angrily onto the top rack.

"To be fair, I did tell her a few days ago. She just hadn't met them before now." I looked down at the bottle of gin in my hand and added another healthy dollop to the pitcher. "When would I have had time to tell anyone?"

Jaqi didn't look at me as she added another bowl to the dishwasher. "You could have told us as soon as you got home. Honestly, Vee, sometimes you make me feel like we don't even matter. It's like nobody exists but you."

I opened my mouth to say something but what was there to say? She was right, I hadn't even thought to tell them, and there had been plenty of time before dinner.

"I'm sorry Jaqi, you're right. I'm a lousy friend sometimes. My only excuse is that I still hadn't processed it. Bee had had children, and she just walked away from them. I still can't believe it."

Jaqi nodded, although she still didn't look happy. "I get it; I would be freaked out too." She closed the dishwasher door and poked a couple of buttons. Then she turned to lean her hip on the counter and stared me right in the face. "That really doesn't sound like the Bee we knew, does it? I would never have thought she'd keep a secret that big, I mean, that she would even have had one."

DAWN WAS JUST BREAKING, and I could hear the first few brave birds singing outside the kitchen window. I hadn't turned on very many lights, only the one over the stove, and it was still dim in the little breakfast nook. I didn't want anyone to know that Miko had slipped me the case file on Bee's death. There it sat in the middle of the table in front of me, a bright yellow folder on grey Formica.

I knew I was stalling. Seeing the cold, clinical language the cops used to describe death would make it so real, so sad. Despite having gotten up at 4:00 a.m. in order to read it, I couldn't even force my hands to open the folder.

Instead, I carried my cooling coffee to the microwave to reheat it. *Maybe I should make something to eat; I always think better on a full stomach.* I just didn't have much of an appetite these days, as was becoming clear from how loose my pants were. If Luci noticed I was losing weight, she would go mama bear all over me, and I just couldn't face that. Not right now.

Okay, I was definitely letting the sad secrets I'd been learning affect my mood. Everyone had secrets, each more depressing than the last. I could feel that black dog nipping at me and sapping my will to do anything but sit and contemplate the pointlessness of human existence. Which was pretty sad on its own. Even Ben had noticed I seemed thinner, at least I suspected he had, since he had kept slipping me extra treats and cream-based soups every time I saw him.

Worst of all, I was losing my loving image of Aunt Bee. The more I learned, the less she seemed like the woman I'd known. I had never suspected Bee had so many secrets, or that she had caused as much difficulty for others as they had caused for her when she had transitioned. I could almost see their point, changing one's gender had been nearly unheard of in the 50s. And people being people, any confusion or disruption to their worldview would've resulted in a lot—and I mean a lot—of pushback. I had always thought her the bravest woman. Now I feared she was instead selfish and uncaring.

This saddened me beyond words.

Well, Mom and Aunt Kay would be here within a few minutes.

It was time to stop stalling, fix my makeup, and put on my big-girl panties. The ones with the lace and little bows because I always felt more confident whenever I felt pretty. Sixty years old but Mom just had to give me *that look,* and I became 12 again. I knew that no matter how much discussing Bee's death upset them, it was time for some answers.

I'D BEEN FIGHTING WITH one recalcitrant curl that insisted on pointing straight up when I heard the doorbell ring. Mother was here, and I guess I felt as ready as I'd ever be. I headed down the stairs with one hand on the rail, hopefully to stop me from falling to my death, with Victor bouncing around my feet and barking all the way down. I shook my head; that wasn't even funny to think about.

I opened the door, and my mother stepped in without asking, brushing past me and leaving me damp from her raincoat. Aunt Kay smiled apologetically as she lowered her umbrella and shook it out over the porch before coming all the way in. It was only misting out, but to look at these two, you would think it was a biblical rainstorm. At least, I had managed to convince Mom not to bring food when she was invited for lunch.

Luci had made us paella, rich with tomato, spicy sausages, and shrimp. She called it a simple lunch, but it smelled and tasted like I should be dining in New Orleans' French Quarter. *Huh, maybe when everything settled down a bunch of us should go to New Orleans for a vacation.* Not during Mardi Gras, of course. I was way too peopled out.

I didn't even blame the girls for heading out for the afternoon. I didn't want to be with my mother when she was upset, and I knew I was about to upset her.

I gestured to Mom to sit in the breakfast nook and pulled three plates from the cupboard. I decided to use my fancy china with the silver lace and pink roses, as that would butter Mom up a bit. I needed her in a good mood if she was going to answer any of my questions.

I had picked a few fall flowers from the yard and put them in an old cream pitcher in the center of the table. The grey Formica with chrome edging looked oddly festive with the silver and lace dishes and snow-white cloth napkins. The only jarring note was the large blue soup bowl filled with paella. I made a mental note to buy at least one white tureen so that next time it would match everything else.

My mother noticed these things, although Aunt Kay was more like me, meaning, she didn't care what the table looked like as long as the food was good. And very little compared to Lucia's cooking. I had made sweet iced tea to go with the paella, thinking it would help keep the heat down from the spicy sausages. Luci had trouble with the concept of "too spicy."

All too soon, we cleared our plates and mother tapped her lips with her napkin and set it across her plate. She met Kay's eyes, and Aunt Kay ducked her head, clearly handing responsibility over to my mother for whatever was coming next.

"Victoria, I know why you've asked me here and before you say anything, I have to tell you to stay out of it. Let the police handle things."

"Miko asked me to help. He felt people would talk to me more openly than they would to him, and to be honest, the police have no idea who could've hurt Aunt Bee." I reached over and picked up their plates, quickly piling them on top of mine and carrying them to the sink. I had an overwhelming urge to keep busy.

"I'm sure he was just being polite and didn't expect you to put yourself in danger."

I turned to Mom. She had actually sounded worried about me. I must've said that out loud since she frowned and told me that course she worried about me. Apparently, I was just like my father—too stubborn to know what was good for me, and likely to get hurt because of it.

I wanted to roll my eyes and whine, but that would make me 12 again, and I was way too old to be acting like a tween.

"Mom, you obviously knew Bee much better than I did. Was she fighting with anyone the week before she died? Did she mention being afraid of anyone? Do you have any idea who her stalker was and if they were the same person who was following her back in the 50s?"

She remained silent, only pursing her lips at me in disapproval. Some days her sense of what should be kept private drove me batty.

"Dammit Mom, someone murdered her in cold blood. They don't deserve to get away with it. Help me figure it out."

When her disapproving glare didn't work, Mom turned her gaze to her empty tea glass and rocked it around on the table. Aunt Kay reached over and laid her hand on one of my mother's, stilling it.

"It's not that easy, Victoria," said Aunt Kay. "Bee was a very private woman. She didn't precisely confide in anyone. All I know is that she had begun to worry about the little notes left in her mailbox. She didn't say if they had become threatening, just that they were bothering her. I don't think she ever went to the police about them."

"Aunt Kay, that's the kind of thing I need to know. Did she say who she suspected of leaving them? We've seen on TV how easy it is for a stalker to turn violent if they feel rebuffed. Did she have any angry ex-boyfriends?"

My mom touched Kay's hand to get her attention and shook her head. But Kay shook her hand off and continued to talk to me.

"It's time the secrets were let into the open, Debbie. How do we know it wasn't her secrets that got Bee killed?"

Mom met my eyes for a second and looked away. She had always had a hard time changing her mind about anything, and this was no exception.

"Secrets should remain secret," she said. "That's why they are called secrets."

I reached over and put my hand on hers. There was something about this family and holding hands, but I shook the thought away and pressed on with what had to be said. "Who was she afraid of, Mom?"

Mom shook her head, "I wouldn't have said she was afraid, just... concerned."

I waited a second to see if she would continue and then squeezed her hand. "Who was it?"

"Her neighbor, Burt." Aunt Kay blurted. "She said he was starting to pressure her to go out with him, and he didn't take it well when she refused. Of course, he had no idea why she refused." Kay's face pinked with embarrassment at even hinting at Aunt Bee's transition.

I thought about that. Burt had been very odd that day he broke into my bedroom. I suspected he was in first stages of Alzheimer's, and I knew that later-on Alzheimer's could cause rages, but he wasn't far enough along for that yet, was he?

"Was he the only one she mentioned? Did she mention a man in his 60s?"

"What are you talking about, Victoria? She wasn't seeing any man that young."

IT WAS EARLY EVENING, and I sat on the front porch. The sun was just visible above the trees in the park down the street, and the clouds had mellowed into peaches and pinks with a single jet trail reflecting gold slashing across the layers.

My metal pitcher of martinis was balanced in a salad bowl full of ice cubes on the table beside me, and I had my feet up on the railing. I'd gotten another chapter read in my romance novel, and my brain was starting to wind down from the events of the past few days. Of course, the martini helped. The girls were upstairs talking, and I could hear the occasional giggle float from their open window.

Life was good again.

The couple in the book were just getting around to their first kiss when the back of my neck started itching like I was being stared at. *Not now, this is just getting good.*

Placing my finger at the start of the next paragraph, I glanced up hoping to be mistaken. But no, Margaret stood at the foot of the driveway staring at me.

I swallowed my mild resentment and waved at her to come on down. She had said she was 18, so I couldn't offer her a martini. Ontario drinking laws were very clear that you had to be 19 to drink alcohol.

"Hello, dear. Could I get you anything?" I smiled in a hopefully welcoming fashion while wishing she would go away. I felt so done with people for today.

She shook her head and hunched her shoulders, her hands deep in the pockets of her denim jacket. She put me in mind of one of those ninja turtles.

After a moment, I sighed deeply and set down my glass. "Well then, what can I do for you?"

Margaret shook her head again, and I gestured at the chair on the opposite side of the front door. She might as well sit while she did nothing but stare at me. I picked up my bright, blue martini glass and saluted her with it. "Chin chin."

I admired the water droplets for a heartbeat, then took a sip. *Mmm, delicious.* I had used my fancy bottle of rose-enhanced gin, and it was marvelous.

"I hope you enjoy that while you can." Margaret mustered up a glare. "I've been talking to a lawyer, and he says that since Beatrice inherited Brian Lilley's money, that as Brian's direct descendent, at least half that money belongs to my family, and I'm going to make sure we get it."

Well, this was awkward. Not that I totally disagreed with her, but she could have simply asked. I could feel my temper rising. I never did like ultimatums or threats.

"Why don't we go into the house to discuss it?" I started to stand up, but she waved me back into my seat.

"What, so you can murder me like you did Beatrice?"

I felt my eyes narrow and my brows pinch together. If this kept up, I would start getting wrinkles. Yes, start. I was a fiend for moisturizing, and my skin was soft as a baby's butt.

I must've said that out loud because Margaret smirked muttering *not hardly* under her breath. I felt my frown deepen and made a conscious effort to relax my face. It wouldn't do to let her get under my creamy, white skin. A lady was impervious to the snips and snarls of the envious. And she was clearly envious of my money if nothing else.

The fact that I had been considering giving her and her father half of Aunt Bee's money was irrelevant. She had some nerve coming here and demanding it.

"You can call your lawyer all you want. Beatrice left the money to me, and legally, the money was hers. I don't know what you think you'll get by threatening me."

"You think that was a threat? I haven't even started. You might have my dad fooled, but I'm not that easily taken in by a 'sweet old lady.'" You could hear the quotation marks around *sweet old lady*. The ability to do that must be genetic.

I took another mouthful and swirled the gin around my gums, blowing the fumes out through my pursed lips. It tasted just like my Victoria roses smelled. It was very calming, which was a good thing because I wanted to smack the smirk off of that girl's face. I reminded myself that she was family and only 18, she would grow up someday, and I didn't want to make an enemy of her. So, I took a deep breath and blew it out, trying to think of what to say since I couldn't just tell her the truth. It wasn't my secret to tell.

"Is that all you want, the money? You've been lucky enough to find family where you thought you had none, surely that's worth more than money." I watched her turn her head to stare at her feet and scuff at a mark on the cement porch. After a moment she shrugged again.

"I guess it's easy not to care about the money when you have it all. My dad's family grew up with nothing. Now I have the choice of going into serious debt to go to college or working at a crummy job for the rest of my life. How would you feel?"

The child did have a point.

"But you don't have to threaten me; you could just talk to me. I'm not that frightening am I?" But a thought started to niggle in my brain:

If it was all about the money, how desperate was she to get it? How far would she go?

I had always managed to have enough for my needs, mostly by keeping my needs simple. I couldn't understand the desperation and jealousy that would lead someone to kill over money, but I knew it happened way too often.

"You don't understand! You with your martinis and your rare-breed dog, you've probably never been hungry a day in your life. When you can't afford gas for the car, money means everything. You don't know what people will do for money unless you've been there."

Then her words crystallized a nagging feeling in the pit of my stomach. Had she just confessed to Bee's murder? How much danger was I in right now? She'd pulled her hands out of her pockets, but they were still clenched into fists on her lap and her cheeks had flushed pink with anger.

With that, Margaret got up and kicked at the cement pot of pansies and petunias at the edge of the stairs. I could tell she'd hurt her foot by the way she half-limped down the stairs. *But seriously, who kicks a cement pot?*

Before she reached the road, she was already running. I picked up my phone from beside the salad bowl of ice. I should call Miko, but how to explain the feeling in my gut?

AUNT BEE HAD BEEN BURIED for a week now, and we were finally ready to hold the memorial.

Ben had brought her favourite marzipan-filled croissants and a commercial sized pot of her favourite tea, the one with the oranges and cinnamon.

The priest arrived, but I guess there was nothing we could have done about that because Greta had invited him. They sat together on the loveseat, wearing matching scowls. Perched on a hard chair was the Father's assistant, a sour looking woman of indeterminate age.

Mark and Margaret stood together uncomfortably by the stairs. Neither one acted like they wanted to be here, but neither one seemed like they were willing to leave. I still hadn't decided what to do about them. Well, with him, since I felt certain Margaret was the killer.

Luci and Jaqi walked straight into the kitchen from the side door leading to the driveway. Luci had brought Arroz con Pollo, and Jaqi carried two bottles of that sweet German wine that Helen had served. I guess Luci'd decided she liked it. Soon we would have a full buffet.

Now if Miko could only get here, I'd be ready to reveal the killer. It was bad enough I had to figure it out, but I couldn't actually arrest her. Where was a man when you needed one?

The doorbell rang, sending Victor into fits of barking. I hated to use my cane in the house, but it did come in handy for tapping people's feet to make them move.

By the time I got to the door, Helen had already answered it. Miko entered with a grim expression and nodded at me where I stood in hallway. He gave me a questioning stare, then shook his head.

What did that mean? It didn't matter; I was going to unmask the killer, and Miko was here to arrest them. Aunt Bee would get justice, and nothing else mattered.

Luci had insisted that first we eat, then we could fight with killers. Order was very important to her.

I sat on the couch, my eyes flitting from one person to another as I woodenly shoveled food into my face. How would they react when I unmasked the killer? Did anyone actually know anyone? I had thought that Bee's offspring and I had started to get along, but now I saw them as greedy liars. And at least one was a killer.

Someone tapped my knee, and I nearly dropped my plate. I guess I had been thinking harder than I realized. I looked up.

It was Father Murdock with a most serious gaze. "Would you like me to start things off with a prayer?"

"Why would I want that?" I hadn't meant to be so rude, but my mouth spoke without me again. "I mean, you said a prayer at her re-internment whether I wanted you to or not." *Hot-dogs, that was still rude.* I smiled, "I mean, you know neither of us are Catholic. Although I'm sure the Catholics here were very comforted."

He didn't seem impressed. He looked even less impressed when Jaqi opened the wine and started pouring glasses for people. Burt wandered in from the kitchen with an open beer bottle and decided to help Jaqi hand out the wine.

The bleached out looking woman beside the minister took a glass of wine, and the minister frowned as she downed it in one go. My opinion of her went up. I wondered what her name was. It would be easy to find out; she was the church secretary or something.

Jaqi handed me a large glass of wine. I guess she had run out of smaller glasses.

Well, everyone's present, so I might as well get started.

I caught Miko watching me I as I levered myself to my feet.

"I guess you're all wondering why you were called here. I would like to tell you I have good news, but I can't. No matter how you look at it, Bee was murdered by someone she knew and trusted." I heard my voice roughen with emotion.

I saw Burt come out of the kitchen with a slice of cake, and I briefly wanted one. I wondered who else was in the kitchen, and if they could hear me. I raised my voice anyway.

I pointed dramatically at Margaret where she sat uncomfortably, rolling a glass of soda back and forth in her hands. Everyone stared at her.

"What?" Margaret looked equal parts scared and confused.

"You don't have to say anything, I know what you did."

Now everyone was confused except for Burt, Miko, and the girls.

"I didn't do anything," said Margaret. "Except those stupid roses, and you caught me already." She stared at her dad, her eyes wide and nervous looking. He shook his head at her.

I could hear people whispering behind me, but I kept my attention on Bee's grandson and great-granddaughter. I felt bad for them, but no matter how hard a hand life had dealt, they had no right to kill Aunt Bee.

I raised my voice to be heard over the whispering and ploughed ahead. From the corner of my eye, I saw Miko shake his head and start toward me.

Chapter Thirteen

"**D**id you hear me? I said I know what you did," I repeated louder. Margaret just shook her head.

"I know you killed Bee," I insisted. "I just don't know why." I heard a noise from the kitchen, but figured it was someone moving to the door to listen. "I don't know how you got her to take the pills either."

"What pills? I don't know what you're talking about! I didn't do it!" The girl looked genuinely confused and upset.

I heard Miko clear his throat and glanced behind me. He had his gun out, which seemed a little premature, as Margaret wasn't trying to run.

"Well, arrest her. She had opportunity and she definitely wanted Bee's money." But Miko wasn't looking at me or Margaret; his gaze was fixed on the kitchen.

I turned to the half wall and saw a terrified Ben. My eyes moved slowly from his face, to the butcher knife pressed against his throat, then up to the face of the person standing behind him.

Greta.

Why is she holding Ben? He didn't murder Aunt Bee, Margaret did. Right?

Helen took a couple of steps toward the short wall. "Greta, what are you doing?"

"What does it look like?" She gestured at Miko with the hand that gripped Ben. "Drop the gun, or he's dead."

126

Miko just shook his head and kept the gun trained on Greta.

"Do you think I'm kidding? I have nothing to lose, and they say the first time's the hardest. This is not my first time."

"Greta, put that down. What are you thinking?" Helen wrung her hands and glanced at Miko, who still pointed his gun at Greta. "You always make everything worse."

"What am I thinking?! What were *you* thinking?" Greta tugged Ben toward the shelter of the fridge. "That she would love you? That you would leave me? Never going to happen. Oh yes, I heard you two talking. You were thinking of leaving me. I couldn't have that."

I could feel my jaw drop, Greta had never struck me as unbalanced before, but I was beginning to wonder.

"You don't understand, Greta." Helen's eyes shone with tears, "I loved Bee."

Greta sneered, her face suddenly cruel and vicious looking. "And you thought she loved you back." She made a scoffing noise, but meaner. "She never loved you. She put up with you. Just like Frank, she would have left you."

"What does Frank have to do with it?" Helen's face was white, and her hands shook.

Greta tugged at Ben and a drop of blood slid from under the knife. She glared at Miko. "I'm still watching you, so don't you even try it."

I inched toward the hallway where I could reach the kitchen. I don't know why; someone would have to go in the back door to surprise her. Everyone was out here, where she could keep an eye on them.

I leaned on my cane, sliding one foot closer to the hall. The minister, helpful as always, stood up to give me his chair. What a pumpernicle poopy. All he'd done was gain Greta's attention.

"Don't you move either, Vee. Don't think I don't know what you're trying to pull. I know all about what you've been up to."

"Greta, please, tell me about Frank," cried Helen. "What did you do?" She didn't seem to see anyone but Greta.

I slid a little further down the hall and motioned for the Minister to sit the hell down.

"What do you think I did?" barked Greta. "He was going to take you away from me. I heard you talking. And I knew his life insurance would pay off the house." Greta's hands tightened on the knife and on Ben. Another drop of blood dripped toward his collar. "I told you I would take care of you, and I did."

Helen's voice quivered, "You killed him? You killed my husband?"

"What did you think? Did you think it was a real accident? That he just fell asleep at the wheel?" Greta laughed in a creepy sort of way.

We must have resembled a frame from a movie or a photograph of a crime scene. Greta and Ben in the space above the half wall, the rest of us staring at her with our mouths open.

It had never even occurred to me to question Helen's widowhood. Why would it? And if Frank had fallen asleep while driving, had Greta drugged him with the same pills she'd given Aunt Bee?

How did she think she was going to get away with it all? I supposed she could duck out the back door, if she could run fast enough to get away from everyone. She was certainly in good enough shape.

I realized I'd been talking out loud when Greta laughed.

"You really think they'll jump me while I have him?" She jerked Ben closer to her chest and eased back toward the door.

Miko took a step forward, but Greta shook her head at him.

"Put the gun down, hero. You wouldn't believe the mess slitting his throat would make."

Miko and Greta stared at each other for a moment, and then Miko raised one hand and carefully placed the gun on the coffee table.

"Not there, toss it in here. But be careful not to hit me or my hand might slip." She laughed wildly and Miko's face paled. He picked up the gun by the barrel and gently tossed it toward the half wall. It hit the wall just below the wooden mantle and fell to the floor with a loud thump. It was under two dining chairs and would be difficult to get out in a hurry.

Greta leaned forward a bit to see where the gun had gone, and Ben moved his hands to grip the arm holding him. But that was all he managed to do as she jerked him backward, closer to the outside door.

"Everyone just stay where you are! Vee thinks you are all her friends, so let's see which one of you gets this boy killed."

I could barely breathe and glancing around, I saw everybody frozen in fear. No one had answered the question of how we would get out of this. It was up to me.

God help us all.

Chapter Fourteen

Pulling Ben with her, Greta stepped closer to the outside door. No one had dared move to stop her.

She let go of Ben to reach behind and open the door, although the knife remained at his throat. I could see the moment she realized the door pulled in instead of pushing out. Her own body blocked the door, keeping it shut.

Greta spat a couple of curse words not for delicate ears. While Greta's attention remained on shuffling them both so she could escape, Miko moved closer to the dining room chairs where the gun lay. Greta didn't seem to notice, so he took another step.

A pinky-brown blur raced for the kitchen.

"Victor, no!" My brave little boy was trying to save Ben, but what could a tiny Chihuahua do?

Victor barked furiously, practically bouncing up and down with the force of it. Greta kicked at him, but thankfully missed.

"Get this ankle biter away from me!"

Victor must've taken pride in her cursing him because he promptly bit her ankle. Greta yipped loudly. She tried to kick my dog again, but he growled and dove in for another nip.

While she was distracted, Miko had managed to grab his gun and was leaning on the half-wall, pointing it at her.

"Freeze!"

Greta looked up at Miko, and a horrible expression crossed her face. I just knew she was about to do something terrible.

"You think you've won. You don't know anything." I saw her arm flex as she made to pull the knife across Ben's throat.

Just as we all thought he was a goner, the door was thrown open hard and hit Greta in the back. She stumbled forward, loosening her grip on Ben. He immediately spun on one foot and punched her in the face. Greta went down.

Luci stepped into the kitchen through the back door and looked down at Greta. Greta held the side of her face but still reached for the knife she had dropped. Miko yelled at everyone to freeze, but instead, Ben bent to grab the knife, and Luci leapt on Greta, grabbing her wrists.

Miko ran for the kitchen, pushing people out of his way, and pointed his gun at Greta. She finally froze.

Pretending a bravery I did not feel, I pulled my phone out of my bra and dialed 911. As I explained the situation, a loud thump sounded behind me.

I turned to find Helen lying on the floor, her face far too white and her body far too still. I yelled into the phone for an ambulance and didn't wait for a response. I shoved my phone at whoever was standing next to me and quickly knelt by Helen's side.

She was still breathing.

THINGS WERE A BLUR after that. People yelled and jostled about and everyone spoke at once.

I didn't notice the ambulance or the police arrive; they were just suddenly there. I only saw them when an EMT pushed me away from Helen to attach the leads from a portable heart monitor to her chest. I moved to her other side but was again pushed away by a different EMT who hooked up an IV bag. He was talking into a mic clipped to his collar and seemed to be relaying stats and comments to the dispatcher.

That was fine with me; I only hoped they were in time. Helen was so still, so small, so pale.

Once they loaded Helen upon a stretcher and pushed it out to the ambulance, Miko called to the second EMT to wait. He nodded at me but continued to push Helen down the stairs and out.

A few moments later, Miko returned and made his way to the kitchen. I could hear Ben protesting that he was perfectly fine and just needed a Band-Aid.

Miko wouldn't stand for it, and soon Ben was loaded up into the ambulance

Chapter Fifteen

Ben was fine. He had only needed a few stitches. I walked out of his room into the corridor and glanced around. I could see the police down at the end of the hall standing outside of a door and talking to a man in a white coat. That must be the doctor in charge of Greta, I wondered if anyone watched Helen and where her room was.

The nurse's station was in the other direction, so I headed down that way. I hated the way my walker squeaked as I pushed forward and wondered if the nurses had any grease or lubrication for the wheels. *Would KY jelly work? They must have that.*

They didn't, but they did give me Helen's room number. It was only two doors down from Ben's, and I was surprised I hadn't seen her as I passed by. I squeaked my way back to room 212 and saw the door closed. I knocked quietly in case she was asleep, or a doctor was in there with her. There was no response, so I eased the door open and peered in.

Helen was asleep. Wires crisscrossed the space between her and a bank of beeping machines. I wished I knew what the numbers meant. She seemed to be sleeping comfortably, so I decided the numbers weren't too horrible. Could I use my cell phone in here, or would it mess up the machines?

I decided to wait for her to wake up, so I pulled up the only visitor's chair and sat. From here, I could still see the monitors and decided to risk looking up the numbers.

It turned out that they were very promising, only her heart rate was a little high. I leaned over to snag her chart from the foot of her bed but didn't understand a word of the chicken scratching, abbreviations, or stats. I placed it back on the foot of her bed, well below where her feet could reach—I didn't want her kicking it off the bed. And I settled in to wait.

I had just dozed off when the door opened, and a far too cheerful nurse came in. She had a warm, dark brown complexion and had a musical lilt to her voice.

"And how is everyone doing today? Resting comfortably?" Her words woke Helen up with a start and me with a jerk. My hip spasmed, and I almost fell from the chair. My gasp of pain alerted the nurse to my presence in the shadows. She looked over at me and smiled. "And we have a visitor. What's your name, dearie?"

"Victoria. What's yours, sweetie?" I knew I was being a bit sharp, but I was never my best soon as I woke up, and her cheerfulness certainly did not help.

Helen glanced from the nurse to me then asked for some water. The nurse murmured what I assume was comforting phrases and picked up the empty water pitcher and left the room.

"Vee, is that you?"

"Yes it's me. I thought I'd drop by and make sure you were okay. How are you holding up?" I moved closer to the head of the bed and reached out to place my hand over hers.

"I feel like a truck parked on my chest, but I'm alive. Was it a heart attack? My doctor warned me I was at risk. I was supposed to stay away from stress." She shifted on the bed, her face creasing into a frown.

I glanced toward the door to see if the nurse would return, but there was no sign of her. I pushed my walker as close to the bed as it would go and tried to help Helen sit up higher.

She was heavier than she looked, and I struggled to shift her. As I put my weight fully onto my right leg in order to reach across the bed, my leg gave out. I lost my balance, falling heavily onto the walker.

The nurse walked back in just as I slid off my walker and onto the floor, one hand still gripping the bed-rail.

"What are you doing?" She hurried over to Helen, checking to make sure the leads were still attached. She then bustled around the end of the bed to me.

I was a bit shaken; it had been a long time since I've fallen.

"I'm alright, stop fussing." I batted at the nurse's hands as she tried to help me to my feet. She kept trying to get her hands under my arms to lift me straight up, which I knew from experience was a bad idea.

Eventually, I got the walker around between us and pushed her away with it. After glaring at me, she rounded the bed to help Helen sit up. It turned out the bed was automatic, and I could've just pushed the bright red button.

Oops.

I SAT ON THE EDGE OF the chair, holding Helen's hand. She was still so pale that I worried about her. Her grip felt stronger than expected, though, and she kept asking about Greta.

I really did not want to visit Greta; I had nothing to say to her. I didn't want to hear what she had to say either. Her actions had said it all.

"Vee, please. I need to know what she did to Frank. He was never going to leave me, that's why he was getting the house ready to sell. We were moving to the Maritimes for his job."

"Greta didn't say he was leaving you, she said you were leaving her. I guess you didn't hear her too well what with the heart attack happening and everything."

I could tell by the look on her face she still wanted me to go, and I guess I had a couple of questions of my own. *Like, "What the hell?"* And had she given him the same pills she'd given Aunt Bee? Since she had said he fell asleep at the wheel, it made sense.

I patted Helen's hand and nodded. I would go.

"I don't know what I'm going to do if she goes to jail," said Helen.

"If?" I shook my head—there was no *if* about it. After holding a knife to Ben's throat, Greta would definitely go to jail.

"I just don't know; I've never lived alone. What would I do with myself? Especially in my condition." Helen rubbed a hand across her face, I think she was crying.

It must be left over from years ago, but I just can't deal with a woman crying. Patting her hand didn't seem to help, and there wasn't much else I could do. Except for the one thing she wanted.

Chapter Sixteen

I limped my way down the hall toward two cops I didn't recognize. This would've been easier if it had been Constable Smith. Who knew what MacGuinty might've told them about me? That man detested me, and the feeling was mutual.

I got the cold *cop-stare* when it became obvious I was headed for Greta's room. The older cop stepped in front of me to bar my way. I tried to smile like I was harmless and possibly lost.

"I'm Greta's next-door neighbor. Is she up to visitors?"

He stared at me for a second before answering, "She's under arrest."

"I'm not here to break her out." I gestured at my walker. "I promised her sister I'd check on her." I pointed back down the hall toward Helen's room. "She's had a heart attack, and I don't want to upset her."

The cops looked at each other and had a silent conversation. I was pretty sure I could follow what they were thinking just by their gestures and the way they raised their eyebrows.

They were not going to let me in.

If there is one thing I dislike, it's being told no. Especially if I didn't want to do something in the first place.

"Who ordered you to be here? Because Detective Shiomi told me I could visit her." I had my fingers crossed under the handle of my walker, where I hoped they couldn't see them.

After much muttering and a quick call to Miko, who did not give me away, I was told I had five minutes. A lot can get done in five minutes.

I WOULDN'T SAY GRETA was pleased to see me, or that she answered my questions, but a lot can be told from what one does not say.

For instance, she only gritted her teeth when I asked her if she had been following me. But she grinned smugly when I asked about the toy dog.

"Greta, what happened to your husband? Didn't you say you were married?"

"He died of cancer. What do you think I am, a monster?"

She really didn't want the answer to that question, but I saw no reason to be rude. I still had more questions. And about two minutes left.

"What about Bee, Greta? Helen thinks you killed her as well as her husband." That did not come out right; let me try again. "I mean, she thinks you killed Bee, and her own husband."

Greta glared at me for a moment, then turned her head to the wall. If she thought that was enough of a dismissal to get rid of me, she was mistaken. I was tempted to grab her chin and forced her to look at me but decided that was a bad idea.

"I need your answer, and I'm not leaving until I get it."

Greta turned her head to glare at me some more. I glared back, and I think I won because she resumed speaking.

"All right, I did murder your stupid aunt. She thought I didn't know she was planning to take Helen away from me. I couldn't let that happen, you understand. So, I gave her a few of my sleeping pills."

"Helen said that her husband fell asleep driving to get her. Did you give him the same pills?"

Greta laughed. "Not the exact same pills, of course. I killed him years ago. It was a different prescription."

"But you killed them both, and you're not even sorry?"

"I couldn't let Helen leave. She's all I have. And that's all I have to say. Get out."

"I can't believe you murdered my aunt. I wish we still had the death penalty."

"What are you complaining about? You got everything she ever had. You've never had it so good, and it's all thanks to me." She laughed again.

I felt tears prick, though whether anger or sorrow, I had no idea. I turned and hurried from the room. Let the cops deal with her, she was going nowhere.

I had a lot to think about as my walker squeaked my way back to Helen's room. The only time Greta had answered a question was when I asked about Helen. Even then, her answer was that Helen was hers, and Bee couldn't have her.

I wondered what could have gone wrong in their childhood that created one sister's bond made of love, and the others of obsession.

I tapped gently at Helen's door before opening it. I heard her call for me to come in, so I did.

Chapter Seventeen

A week later, I went back to the hospital. Greta was in jail, awaiting trial. Everyone who had been at the memorial was told to hold themselves available for questioning.

We had also been told not to speak of it among ourselves, but that hadn't stopped anybody. In fact, I think Burt had hosted a party just to talk about what had happened.

Luci was still at my place. She and Jaqi had not yet completely patched up their differences. I so hoped they would work things out because I really did hate it when the kids fought.

The nurses all knew me by now. I was waved past their desk and didn't have to sign in. I guess I had been here enough times, but poor Helen had lost everything, and I really felt for her.

I couldn't let her go back to an empty house. Her big sister had always looked after her, and she had never lived alone. It was all too much of a change, too much of a shock.

I hoped I wasn't going to regret this.

Tapping lightly at Helen's door, I pushed it open and leaned in. The same nurse as I'd seen on that first visit was helping her pack. Helen didn't have much, just a few things I had brought her to make her comfortable.

Helen looked up at me as the door squeaked, and smiled. The nurse tossed the last two items into the bag and zipped it shut.

She nodded as she eased past me and left the room. I leaned my head back into the corridor to ask if Helen could leave now, but the nurse shook her head.

"The doctor still hasn't signed her out. But he should be here very soon."

Helen sat on the bed, and I sat on my walker. We just watched each other for a moment until Helen sighed loudly.

"I suppose I just go home now." She looked smaller than she used to, more fragile. I couldn't let her be alone.

"You could always stay with me. I'm sure I have room." I had no idea why I said that. But it did seem like a good idea.

"Oh, I couldn't. I don't want to be a bother." But her smile said otherwise.

"I won't hear a word about it. Luci will be going home soon, and that will leave the guest bedroom free. I'll make you up the couch for now, so you don't have to climb stairs."

I could see her eyes glimmer with tears and hoped they were happy tears. She nodded and patted her little bag.

"We will have to stop at my house for a few more things. I don't have any clean clothes."

I missed living alone, I'd grown to love just worrying about myself and eating what I wanted when I wanted. Still, I would ask the doctor how long she had to stay, or when she could be left on her own at home. It couldn't be more than a few weeks at most.

This would work out fine.

Right?

<<<>>>

Also by Delilah Knight

Miss Vee Mysteries
Miss Vee and the Lecherous Lawyer
Miss Vee and the terrible trailer park
Miss Vee and Bee's Betrayal

Watch for more at www.delilahknight-author.com.

About the Author

Delilah Knight is the pen name of author Laurie Stewart. Where Laurie writes sci-fi and fantasy, her alter-ego writes light and entertaining cozy mysteries.

Both contain main characters who are disabled, LGBT+, or over 50. Sometimes all three.

Read more at www.delilahknight-author.com.